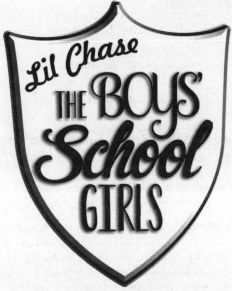

Lil Chase
THE BOYS' School GIRLS

Abby's Shadow

Quercus

First published in Great Britain in 2015 by

Quercus Editions Ltd
55 Baker Street
7th Floor, South Block
London
W1U 8EW

A CIP catalogue reference for this book is available
from the British Library

Paperback ISBN: 978 1 78206 982 9
Ebook ISBN: 978 1 84866 818 8

1 3 5 7 9 10 8 6 4 2

Typeset in Perpetua by Nigel Hazle
Printed and bound in Great Britain by Clays Ltd, St Ives plc.

For my brother and sister,
who were brave.

Chapter 1

My uncle turns the corner and we're finally on my street. I don't like this time of year; it's only 4 p.m. and it's already getting dark. I've been away for the week of half-term, but so much has happened it feels like a month. I'm not really sure if I'm the same person I was when I left. It'll be nice to get back to normal.

I can't wait to see my sister. I can't wait to see my parents. I can't wait to see the surprise that Tara's left on my doorstep.

'Do you know if Mum and Dad are home yet?' I ask my aunt Jenny. She's been calling Mum every few hours since Mum, Dad and Becky left our holiday in a rush.

Jenny turns awkwardly to look back at me from the passenger seat. She shakes her head. 'Sorry, honey, they're still at the hospital.'

I nod like I understand. And I *do* understand, but that doesn't mean I'm thrilled about it.

Jenny clearly picks up on my look and says, 'But your uncle and I will stay with you tonight. We can even get takeaway if you want.' She raises her voice like she's trying to excite a baby. 'Whatever you'd like.'

This is how they always make it up to me. Shove me full of takeaway and treats as if that's the same as having a family who are together. Becky gets my parents, and I get fat.

'I'm not hungry.'

Immediately I feel guilty for sulking. I wouldn't trade places with Becky for anything. No one would. And I wouldn't swap with my parents either: having a child so sick that she's rushed to hospital every few months must be awful. It means Mum can't work and Dad has to work twice as hard. Almost the only time they get to spend with each other is when they're at Becky's bedside – hardly a romantic date.

Doesn't change the fact that I'm the one left out.

My phone beeps:

You still coming home tonight? Don't want the surprise on your doorstep to be stolen by squirrels ☺ *x x*

Tara! She'll make me feel normal again. I wonder what she's got me. Maybe she's written me a long letter like she used to before we both got mobiles. Maybe it's make-up. Or maybe she's got some info on Joel. Maybe she's found out from Reece that Joel likes me back.

'Who was that?' asks Jenny.

'Tara,' I tell her. 'She's bought me a present.'

We're turning on to our drive and I crane my neck between my aunt and uncle to see if I can see what's there. But my phone beeps again so I look down at the display:

Yoooohoooo!

It's Tara again. What does *yoohoo* mean?

'It's Tara!' shouts Jenny.

'That's what I was . . .' But when I look up

I see what she means; there's Tara. She's sitting on my doorstep, in the dark, waiting for me. And it's the best present ever.

I barely wait for my uncle to stop the car before opening the door and jumping out. Tara's got her arms wide open and we have a massive hug.

'Abs! I'm so glad you're back! I've missed you so much!' she yells.

'Me too!' I yell back.

We bounce around in circles hugging each other, and everything's back to how it should be. She's still the same old Tara – long brown hair, smiley and fun. I'm still the same old me too.

'What's been going on round here?' I ask her. 'What's the goss? Everything OK with you and Reece?' Reece and Tara only started going out this week . . . but a lot can happen in a week! 'I can't believe I wasn't around to see you and him finally get together.'

Tara's face can't help but light up at the sound of Reece's name. 'It's great. He's great. We're greatness.' Then her face falls.

'But we can talk all about that later. How's Becky?'

There's a lump in my throat. It pops up so quickly, like it's always there but only rises to the surface when I have to say the words out loud.

Tara's jaw clenches.

'She started getting really sick on holiday,' I tell her. 'Then the other night Mum woke me up to say they were going back to London to take her to hospital.'

I was fast asleep on the foldaway bed when Mum came in, fully dressed, her hair all a mess. It wasn't the first time it's happened, but this time we were in a little holiday cottage in Wales. There was a hospital in Wales – obviously – but Becky had to go all the way back to London where her specialists are, the team of people who have been treating Becky since she was a baby when they realized something was up with her kidneys.

Mum had told me to go back to sleep and enjoy the rest of my holiday – I deserved it. I did go back to sleep. And I did enjoy my holiday. Does that make me a terrible person?

'It's a bad one,' I tell Tara.

Tara doesn't bother saying the things other people always say: *It'll all work out . . . Doctors can work miracles*, etc., etc. She used to, because we all used to believe it. But Becky's been ill for so long we don't believe those things any more. Doctors are great and they do their best, but they're just human like the rest of us.

Instead Tara gives me another hug.

'If you want, I could stay the night,' she says, looking over to my aunt and uncle.

Uncle Wesley is showing off, trying to carry as many bags out of the car as he can. Jenny is clutching a food chest.

She smiles at Tara. 'Of course, Tara. You're always welcome to stay.'

'Yesssss!' we both say at exactly the same time.

'And we can still get takeaway?' I ask.

Jenny nods and shoos us into the house. 'I'll order the usual – you still like ham and mushroom?'

We nod and race upstairs, turning all the lights on as we go. I hate the dark. And coming back to the dark, empty house without Becky is the worst.

As soon as we close my bedroom door Tara jumps on to my bed and sits there cross-legged.

'Sooooo,' she says, 'how was your holiday then? You said in your texts you were having a pretty good time.'

I clamber up opposite her. 'It was good.' I lower my voice in case Jenny and Wesley can hear. 'Thing is, my aunt and uncle are more dog people than children people, so after Mum and Dad left, I could do pretty much what I wanted.'

'Cool!' says Tara, her brown eyes twinkling. 'So . . . spill.'

'Umm, nothing to spill, really.' I don't want to tell Tara what I got up to.

'Stop holding out on me!' she says, shoving me on the shoulder. 'Did you meet any cute boys?'

What happened on holiday doesn't matter. It was so far away that it doesn't feel real. I avoid the question by saying, 'None as cute as Joel.' So I don't have to go into it.

'Did you make any friends?'

'No,' I say. But this is a little white lie. Like I said, it doesn't matter now.

'Oh . . .' Tara's frowning now. 'So what *did* you do then?'

'You know, just chilled out.'

Not true. But I was a different person when I was there and I'm not sure she'll want to hear about it.

'You must have done something!' she says.

'It wasn't that much fun really. I'm just glad I'm back with my BFF.'

'Me too,' she says. She holds up her wrist and flashes her bracelet at me. I gulp.

'Hey!' She reaches forward and grabs my wrist. 'Where's my Best Friend Friendship bracelet?'

I'm still wearing the bracelet the girls in Year 8 wear. Our school – Hillcrest High – was a boys' school until the beginning of this term when they admitted ten girls to our year. Ten girls versus hundreds of boys. That's if you include Simone, who doesn't hang out with us for some reason. We always say hello and wave to her, but she never responds. But the rest of us nine have all become really good friends. We decided to form the Boys' School Girls and we always stick together. No matter what. Candy made us matching scoobies so we never forget it.

But Tara and I have known each other much longer than the others – she's been my best friend since we were four – and we made each other matching *Best Friend* friendship bracelets. We even bought silver discs that say '*Best Friends*' and threaded them into the strings.

Tara's wearing hers. Mine's gone.

'It's in my suitcase,' I tell her. 'It kept coming off. The clasp broke.'

But this too is a lie.

Quickly I change the subject. 'Will you come and see Becky with me tomorrow?'

Tara frowns a little and she clenches her teeth. 'It depends – what time? Because the thing is I'm meeting Reece tomorrow. Oh, Abby, he's amazing. We've kissed once or twice and it's amazing. He's a really good kisser. We don't snog every day, but . . .'

And we're back to normal: Tara talking about her stuff while I smile like a devoted best friend.

Only it doesn't make me feel good, and it doesn't make me relax. Maybe because I'm not really listening.

Why did I tell her the bracelet was in my bag? Why didn't I tell her that I lost it? That would have been so much cleverer! Now I've lied to my best friend. And it feels bigger than a little white one. It's a dirty great big one.

Chapter 2

When Mum and Dad said we were going on holiday for the autumn half-term I was stupid enough to get my hopes up. We don't go on holiday that much because we have to be near a hospital that will do Becky's regular dialysis. They found one in Wales.

The Pembrokeshire coast is one of those places adults go because it's 'beautiful' and 'picturesque'. But a better way to describe it would have been 'dead' and 'boring'. The most fun I'd had was going for a walk down the beach, maybe stopping in at the post office to buy some sweets and a magazine. Though even the post office was closed more often than it was open. And I was trying not to eat too many sweets.

But there was nothing else to do. Becky was napping and Mum, Dad and my aunt and uncle were doing a crossword together. I headed down there. And of course it started raining.

The holiday cottage was in this little cul-de-sac. As I came out of it I saw some hope – in the form of two really fit boys, both carrying surfboards. One of them was ginger and had his wetsuit open to the waist – even though it was almost November. But if you had a bod like that I guess you'd want to show it off. The other was a bit bigger, with dark hair, and he hid his tummy under his wetsuit. I knew all about hiding my tummy.

I wondered if they'd let me hang out. But how would I even dare to talk to them?

I'll just follow them for a bit, I thought to myself. Is that a bit stalkerish?

I let them get ahead of me as they walked down the road. The wind picked up and made my hair go all over the place. I quickly put it up in a ponytail. The boys were talking and laughing.

I wonder if they've noticed me.

'Not bad, are they?'

I jumped.

When I turned there was a girl sitting on a wall over the road. She had auburn hair, kind of curly and messy, and her face was wet from the drizzle.

'Pardon?' I said.

The girl grinned. Her teeth were a little crooked but actually it made her look quite cute – like she had a cheeky side. I reckoned she was about my age. 'I saw you staring at those boys,' she said, leaping down and crossing the road.

Totally busted! Did I admit it or try to style it out? In the end I went for something in between. 'How old do you reckon they are?'

'How old are you?' she asked me.

'I'm twelve,' I told her. 'Thirteen in January.'

'Ace!' she said. 'Me too.' She scurried forward and walked along beside me. 'I'll be thirteen any second now.'

'Yeah?'

'Yeah,' she said. 'This week, in fact.'

'Umm, happy birthday.'

I tried not to get my hopes up for an invite to a party, but I was totally due for something interesting to happen. While all my friends at Hillcrest were having fun over half-term, it would be so cool if I could have some fun too. Then maybe I wouldn't be Boring Flabby Abby any more. I mean, I'd lost weight, but I was still as dull as this place.

'What's your name?' I asked her.

'Gerry,' she said. 'Short for Geraldine.' She pulled a face.

'Abby,' I said. 'Short for Abigail.' I pulled the same face.

We both laughed.

'And you're here on holiday?' she asked.

I nodded.

'Me too,' she said. 'You an only child as well?'

'I have a younger sister . . .' I wasn't sure whether to tell her the whole deal with Becky. Thing is, whenever I mention it, it becomes a seven-hour story with loads of questions. And there is no happy ending, yet. 'But she's ill,' I finish finally.

'I heard there's a nasty bug going around,' she said. I didn't bother to correct her.

'So, do you want to help me stalk these boys or what?' I asked her.

She smiled at that but said, 'I wouldn't bother.' She threw a glance at them as they walked off into the distance and wrinkled her nose, sizing them up like a new outfit she wasn't sure about trying on. 'They're not really worth it. The ginger one is called Jason. He might have a hot bod but he's such a letch. Always cracking on to me.' She rolled her eyes as if being cracked on to was such a hassle.

I made a look like I was disgusted, but the truth is, no one has ever shown interest in me like that. 'The tubby one – Nick – has an OK personality, but look at him – he's so fat! I wouldn't know whether to kiss him or set up a hog roast.'

'Hey!' I said. 'That's not cool.'

Something dark clouded over Gerry's expression. She glared at me for a second, like I shouldn't be judging her for making a joke. It might have been a joke – but it wasn't a nice one.

'It's just . . . It wasn't long ago that I was fat,' I told her, almost whispering.

'Oh,' she said. The dark look was gone. 'Sorry.'

I carried on walking. Gerry wasn't following me any more and I felt torn: not sure if I wanted to hang out with someone who told mean jokes. But then again, I was stuck in Pembrokeshire for a whole week with no one my age to talk to. Becky's up-and-down health seemed set on *down* – which meant she was in bed, and my parents were right with her. I turned and looked back. I must have imagined the dark expression because now Gerry just looked really sad, like an abandoned puppy.

I smiled at her. 'Are you coming, or what?'

She bounded forward, again like a puppy.

'Come on,' she said. 'I'll show you where they hang out.'

We walked down the steep slope towards the sea, the wind blowing us all over the place. We got all the way to the beach without saying anything. It was a bit awkward because we'd only known each other five seconds and it already felt like we'd had our first fight. The two boys zipped their wetsuits up, then grabbed their surfboards and headed into the water. We sat on the wet sand to watch – it soaked through my denim skirt to my skin but I didn't care.

Finally Gerry spoke. 'I can't believe you were ever fat,' she told me. 'You're so pretty.'

No one had ever called me pretty before.

'Seriously!' she said, clearly picking up on my surprise.

'I have photographic evidence,' I told her. 'Friend me on Facebook and you'll see for yourself.'

Gerry looked down at her ripped-up Converse. 'Umm, I'm not on Facebook,' she said. 'My . . . um . . . dad reckons I'm going to get kidnapped and murdered every time I go on the internet.'

I laughed. 'My parents are the opposite,' I told her. 'I spend my life on Instagram and Facebook but they're so busy they hardly notice. Then they see something on TV that makes them freak out and suddenly they want to go through my friend list and ask how I know them, how old they are, and make sure I'm not meeting up with strangers.' I pulled out my phone. 'Parents are such idiots.'

'Completely stupid!' said Gerry.

I tap the Facebook app. 'Let me show you some pictures of me.' I got to the photo of all of us girls on the very first day at Hillcrest High. Hard to believe it was only a few weeks ago. 'See –' I handed Gerry my phone – 'I'm a giant heifer.'

In the photo Tara had her arm around me. I always used to make sure I was behind someone or something whenever anyone photographed me but even though my body was half hidden by Indiana and Obi, you could see my chubby cheeks.

'You look so different!' she said. Then she looked at me, worried that she'd offended me again. 'I mean, sorry. You looked nice there too but . . .'

'It's OK,' I said, knocking her shoulder with mine so she shuffled forward in the sand. 'I lost a few pounds.'

She scrolled through the rest of my photos. 'Who's that?' she asked.

It was me and Obi, all dressed up for Tara's party. 'It's—' But I hadn't got the words out before she was on to the next one.

'Where are you going there?'

It was me and Tara being silly in hula skirts. Tara's idea.

'We—' But again she didn't give me the time to tell her.

'Who's the band?'

'That's Sucker Punch.' I knew which photo she was looking at: Donna on the mic, set up as their new singer. And Reece on the drums somewhere, hardly visible in the back. Lenny on lead guitar, looking all perfect with his not-a-hair-out-of-place quiff.

'That's Joel,' I told her with a dreamy sigh. He was onstage and hadn't even bothered to iron his T-shirt – but I loved that photo of him. His eyes were closed, getting into the music, his fingers on the guitar strings.

'Are they your friends?' she asked me.

I nodded.

'Wow, Abby,' she said, 'you're so cool.'

I was speechless. No one had ever called me

cool before. Possibly because I wasn't cool. At all. But maybe that could change and I could become a different person. Maybe cool could become a new thing for me.

Time to reinvent Abby.

Chapter 3

The drum roll is so long and loud that I can't really think about anything else. Tara takes my hand and gives it a squeeze, looking at me like, *Isn't my boyfriend amazing?*

Of course Tara thinks Reece is amazing. They've only been going out for five minutes, so everything he does seems perfect. Reece is good at the drums, and he's a nice guy so I'm happy my best friend's with him. But he's not perfect . . . though I'd never tell Tara I think that.

Reece isn't perfect. But Joel is.

Joel looks at me and sticks out his tongue.

I giggle, then lean over to Tara to whisper: 'Wouldn't it be cool if I started going out with my best friend's boyfriend's best friend.'

Tara scrunches up her face and mouths, 'I can't hear you,' tapping her ear as she does.

'WOULDN'T IT . . . ?' But no matter how loud I say it she's not listening – she's back focused on Reece. Never mind, it's a conversation we've had a million times anyway.

'Hold up! Hold up!' Donna's voice pierces through this monumental drum roll and Reece stops playing.

'Thank you!' she says into the microphone with a huffy sigh. She's got her hands on her hips now. 'Reece,' she says, 'you're a great drummer – we all know it – but have you heard the expression *too much of a good thing?*'

Joel and I look at each other and somehow manage not to laugh. But Reece looks outraged at the suggestion, and Tara's backing him up with an equal amount of outrage. It's the first day back after half-term and she's been copying everything he does all day.

'There's nothing wrong with a little drum solo, Donna!' Tara says.

'You're right,' says Lenny, strumming at his guitar. 'There's nothing wrong with a *little* drum solo. That went on for eternity.'

Donna beams at Lenny and we all start

laughing – everyone except Tara and Reece. Tara looks at me but I don't stop. I'm not going to pretend I feel exactly what she does all the time. Not any more.

I guess I have changed a little.

Joel walks over to Reece. 'Sorry, mate.'

Reece lets his grumpy look drop. 'It's OK. I was just trying out some stuff.'

Donna flips her gorgeous hair. 'I think we all know what the problem is here.' She looks over at me and Tara. 'The *group* is being distracted by the *groupies*.' She flips her hair again, as if this makes the statement more true.

'We're just sitting here quietly,' I say, sticking up for myself for once.

'Not being rude, Abby,' Donna says, which usually means she's about to be *very* rude, 'but I don't think *you're* the distraction.'

I'm not insulted though. I've never really thought of myself as a distraction.

Tara grabs me round the waist. 'Aww, Abs,' she says, 'you'll always be a distraction to me.'

I push her off. 'Come on, let's go. If these guys don't hurry up and get famous, how can we say we knew them way back when they were spotty kids.'

'Hey!' says Donna. 'My skin is Clearasil perfect.'

Tara looks at Reece to make the decision for her.

'Go on,' Reece says to her. 'You'd better go. We don't want Diva Donna getting into another one of her strops.'

'Oh, OK,' she says, groaning at the thought of having to part from him for a millisecond. We used to laugh at girls who behaved like this; now Tara's one of them.

She runs over and gives Reece a kiss. 'Keep it clean!' I tell them, and Tara pulls away after just a peck, embarrassed . . . and clearly a bit disappointed that she has to hold off on the snog.

I get up and wait by the door for Tara to grab her things. She gives one last wave to Reece — you'd think he was off to war or something — then she links her arm in mine and we walk out of the music rooms and up the stairs.

In the main corridor we see Obi, Hannah and Indiana.

'Hey, laaaay-deez!' Obi calls at the top of her voice, making the boys in the corridor turn and look.

I blush. I can't help it. I still find it weird being one of the very few girls in a school full of boys. There are only ten of us girls here at the school, including the Secretive Simone. It means we get looked at a lot. Tara and I used to go to a mixed school. But last summer she said she was signing up to Hillcrest, so I said I would too. There's no way I would want to be at a school without her. I thought it would be nice to be surrounded by boys – guaranteed attention! But it drives me mental with paranoia. I pull down the ends of my sleeves and chew them. They're completely wrecked.

'Hey, lay-deez, yourself,' I reply to Obi.

We have a quick hug. 'What are you up to?' she asks us both.

'We've just been watching Sucker Punch while they practise,' I tell them.

'How do they sound?' asks Indiana.

'Amazing,' says Tara. 'Especially the drums.'

'There are a couple of *ego issues*.' I whisper the last two words and the others laugh.

'Donna has always had a massive ego,' says Tara.

'I was talking about Reece!' I say, and nudge her a little so she knows I'm teasing. The girls smile at me and it makes me feel cool. Just like Gerry said I was. Maybe I have always been cool, but I've been hiding it for Tara's sake . . .

Tara's face is set, defensive. 'Speaking of Reece . . .' she starts.

Hannah rolls her eyes.

'I wish I'd never brought him up,' I mumble, and Obi must have heard because she smothers a chuckle behind her hand.

'He sent me the cutest text last night . . .'

'A text?!' Obi says. 'How romantic!'

'Chivalry is still showing vital signs,' says Indiana.

We laugh, but Tara is firmly in the Land of Luuurve and goes on describing the text that he sent her. For a message with ten words in

26

it, she's talking about it like it was a hardback novel.

My phone vibrates and I pull it out of my bag. We carry on walking as I check the screen.

It's a friend request — I haven't had one in ages.

'Oh my God!' I gasp.

It's Gerry! She's finally got herself a Facebook account.

The last time I saw her it was a bit awkward, and on Saturday I sort of ran back to London without saying a proper goodbye. But we already had each other's numbers and had said we'd stay in contact. Two days later and she's done just that.

'What?' asks Hannah.

'It's——' I say.

'. . . which is so funny . . .' Tara says, speaking a little more loudly to cut me off. That's OK. I don't need to tell the others about Gerry. It's not like they'll ever meet her or anything.

'. . . because he usually signs off with a smiley face and then two kisses . . .'

From her profile picture Gerry looks just how I remember. Even prettier, really.

I hesitate for a second. But what's the worst that could happen? I accept her friend request.

'. . . but this time he sends me a load of zs and a sleepy face . . .'

I've tuned Tara out as I start typing a message on Gerry's wall, 'Hi hun, so good to hear from you! How are you? Get me on Instagram too.' And I send her my handle: @Abbracadabra.

'Look, Abby.' Tara shoves her phone under my nose.

'Hey!' I say. 'I'm typing here.' I push her hand away.

Tara frowns. It's not really like me to push her away. Not for anything. 'Who are you texting?' she asks me.

'This girl I met on holiday – Gerry.' I show her Gerry's Facebook picture.

'Oh.'

'She was ace fun,' I tell them.

'*Ace?*' says Indiana.

'Who says *ace?*' repeats Hannah.

28

I laugh. 'It's one of Gerry's words.'

'She looks nice,' says Obi, leaning over to have a look.

'She was *really* nice!' I say. 'And a bit of a wild child.'

Indiana and Obi exchange a look, like they're impressed.

'She lives in north London,' I tell them. 'Barnet somewhere.'

Tara is frowning harder, confused. 'Anyway,' she says, 'I haven't finished telling you about—'

But Hannah cuts her off. 'So your holiday wasn't ruined by your sister getting sick?' she asks me.

'Not completely,' I say. 'Me and Gerry had a really good time.'

'I'm glad,' says Obi. 'You deserve it, with everything your family are going through.'

I *do* deserve it. I *have* been through a lot. I press *Post* on my message to Gerry and we walk along the corridor.

'What happened then?' asks Indiana.

For the first time in ages, all attention is on me. Tara looks hurt that we don't care about her story, but to be honest, she's become a bit boring – every sentence she says seems to have the word 'Reece' in it.

Isn't it about time she listened to what I have to say?

Chapter 4

KNOCK KNOCK KNOCK

The sound at the window made me so scared I dropped the pencil I was drawing with. A million murder scenarios flashed through my mind. I knew I should have kicked up more of a fuss about sleeping downstairs on the foldaway. I was about to become the first to die.

'Only me,' came the whisper from outside.

Gerry.

I didn't know whether to hug her or throttle her! I hid my pad of paper and the photo of Tara I was copying under my pillow. For some reason I didn't want Gerry to see I was drawing a picture of my friend.

As soon as I got to the window, I realized I was wearing my cuddly-bear pyjamas. Cringe!

'God, Gerry!' I whispered back. 'You could have given me a heart attack.'

Gerry laughed. Her face was lit brightly against the deathly dark beyond by the glow from my room, and her hair billowed in the wind.

'I thought *you* might kill *me* if I left you out of this mega party situation,' she said. 'So it was either me or you who was going to die. I chose you.' She laughed again.

I couldn't ignore the p-word. 'What party situation?' My heart started racing.

'Guess!' she said, climbing in through my window without waiting to be asked. 'We're meeting up with the boys.'

I stood back to let her drop in, sitting back down on my bed and covering myself with my pillow so she couldn't see my flabby tummy. 'Which boys?' I asked, though there was only one lot of boys down here – or at least only one pair that we had been stalking for the last four days.

Gerry rolled her eyes. 'Come on!' she said. 'They're meeting us up on the cliff in about . . .' she looked at her wrist where a watch should be, 'two minutes. Get dressed, quick.'

I glanced at the closed door. It wasn't quite eleven yet, but the house was quiet. I wasn't sure about sneaking out at night.

'My parents won't let me go out now,' I told her quickly. 'And they're asleep so I can't ask. Becky hasn't been feeling great since we got here and she's been keeping Mum and Dad up. My aunt and uncle are early-to-bed-early-to-rise types.'

Gerry stuck her tongue out. 'Those types are the worst,' she said. 'Might be voted as prime minister, but would never be voted "most popular".'

'Ha!' I said, then covered my mouth. 'Sorry, I don't think I can come.'

Gerry walked over to my packed suitcase. 'But you just said they're all asleep.' She started rummaging through my clothes. It made me uncomfortable. We'd spent almost all our time together since we met, but she'd never been into the cottage before and I hadn't been to hers – even though her complex sounded much cooler, with a pool and a hot lifeguard on duty. I suddenly realized that I didn't know her that well. I didn't know if she'd laugh at my Minnie Mouse knickers.

I clenched my teeth. Outside looked so dark. 'Umm . . .' I started, but I didn't know how to turn her down. Call for my parents to chuck her out? *Accidently* make too much noise and wake them?

But Gerry was already picking up my bright green lacy top, my jean jacket, and black leggings. She came and sat next to me on the bed, 'I'm sorry your sister is ill, but your parents would want you to enjoy yourself.'

I felt the Becky Lump in my throat and tried to swallow it. I didn't want Gerry to see me cry. That's something only really good friends should witness – what if she laughed at me?

'You're safe if you're with me,' she said.

'I suppose.' I knew my parents worried about me being mugged or kidnapped. 'They've never actually specifically told me not to go meeting boys on cliffs in the middle of the night. But . . .' Truthfully, I was scared. I'd never been a person who did this kind of thing before. 'I don't think I can.'

'But you have to!' she said.

'Sorry,' I said.

'You have to,' she growled.

Her face clouded over. The look was so dark it made me flinch. She must have seen it because she instantly brightened again.

'You have to . . . because it's my birthday!'

'What?! Today?' I'd been with her all day, and she hadn't said a word. 'Why didn't you tell me? I would have made a cake.'

'I hate that sort of attention,' she said, giving a flap of her hand. 'But it's my birthday which means you have to obey me.' Her voice became deep and gravelly. 'I'm ordering you to come.'

Then she grinned so widely I couldn't help but smile back.

'And your parents would think something was wrong with you if you didn't rebel.'

My mum was always saying that worrying about Becky was hers and Dad's job, not mine. 'They do tell me I should concentrate on being a teenager.'

'So let's go be teenagers!' Gerry urged, throwing my clothes at me.

She was right. It was my time to be cool for once. I was always holding back, always in Tara's shadow, waiting for her to tell me what to do. But here there was no Tara to hide behind. Gerry was pushing me . . . in all the right ways.

If I was going to reinvent myself, this was the place to start.

'You don't think I should go like this?' I asked, gesturing at my teddy bear pyjamas.

She looked me up and down, 'I don't think fashion is ready for that kind of statement.'

'Ha!'

She plonked herself on my little bed and didn't look away as I started changing. I was too embarrassed to do it right there in front of her so I moved to the corner and turned my back. Tara was the only person I didn't mind changing in front of, and this felt a bit weird.

'I like that green top,' she said.

It was one of my favourites too. 'Thanks,' I said. 'It's new. From Topshop.' A lot of my stuff was new because of the weight I'd lost.

'And ace bracelets,' Gerry said, pointing to my wrists.

'They're friendship bracelets.' One from the Boys' School Girls, one from Tara.

'Cool.' But she looked a little sad. 'I've never had a friendship bracelet.'

That *was* quite sad. 'I'll make you one before I go,' I said. 'Something to remember me by.'

Gerry's face lit up. 'Thanks!'

Looking at Tara's bracelet gave me a buzz of excitement. She wouldn't have recognized the person I was being just then!

Outside, it was the kind of dark you just don't get in London. The moon was reflecting in the sea, the waves rough in the autumn wind. Gerry led the way. I had no idea where we were going, just that we were meeting the boys on the cliff. I didn't know what scared me more; walking along a cliff in the dead of night, or meeting older boys. I'd never hung out with older boys before. Even surrounded by them at school, boys still freaked me out.

But I was determined to be cool. Just like Gerry thought I was. New, reinvented Abby.

I got out my phone and tapped the torch app.

'Good idea,' Gerry said. She was whispering, even though there was no one around for miles.

The torch only helped a little.

'Hang on,' I said. 'Let's do a photo.' I wrapped my arm around her and held out my phone for a selfie.

She grabbed the phone off me before I could take the picture and said, 'Let me take one of you.' I stuck my tongue out and she clicked, then gave the phone back.

'Now you,' I said. Gerry crossed her eyes, but just at the second I was taking the photo she turned away.

'What's that?'

'What's what?' I replied, suddenly scared again.

'Oh, nothing,' she said, and started walking on.

'Are you sure you know where we're going?' I asked her, trying not to sound nervous.

'Of course I do,' she said. 'It's where I always meet them.'

'And what are their names again?'

'Jason and Nick,' she said. 'Stop worrying, will you?'

Dammit! She realized, even though I'd been trying so hard to hide it. I didn't want to sound like I was scared of sneaking out in the middle of the night, of meeting boys, of . . . well . . . everything. But the path curved dangerously towards the edge of the cliff and I was terrified. Then Gerry started skipping.

'Gerry! Don't!'

She laughed, and skipped higher. Then she stopped. 'There they are!' she hissed.

We rounded some trees and the cliff flattened out to a rough field, with loads of tents and caravans at the far end. In the distance, on the far side of the field, a bonfire was burning. Beside it sat two people. I could see the ends of their cigarettes glowing.

'You don't smoke, do you?' I asked Gerry, whispering now too.

'Nah,' she said. 'I mean, I used to, but I gave up. You?'

I didn't know anyone that smoked. I thought

it was pretty disgusting. 'I've never tried it.' I hoped the boys wouldn't offer me one.

'Good for you.' She was trying to be nice, but it just sounded patronizing.

We opened the gate on to the field and walked towards the boys. In the darkness my phone must have shone as brightly as the moon.

'Who's that?' one of them shouted. I think it was Jason, the ginger one. His voice was really deep. I wondered if it was deep because of the smoking or because he was so much older than us.

Gerry didn't say anything. I looked at her but she just grinned.

'Aren't you going to say hello?' I whispered.

'You shout something,' she whispered back.

'I don't even know them!'

Gerry turned her head so I couldn't see her face.

'Annie, is that you?' Jason shouted again.

'Who're you with?' Nick shouted.

'Not telling!' Gerry yelled, then laughed really hard.

I laughed too. Pure nervous laughter. We were pranking the boys. It felt like flirting.

We were about fifteen metres away before I could see their faces properly, lit by the fire. They were scowling at us, not enjoying being the butt of our joke. If this was flirting, I don't think it was working very well.

'Don't say anything,' whispered Gerry.

'Who are you?' Jason stood up. He looked kind of angry, a little bit threatening.

Nick swore and got up too.

I started to feel a bit sick – a joke's a joke, but they didn't seem to like it. If I waited for Gerry, I knew I might have to wait forever. 'It's Abby and Gerry!' I shouted.

'Abby!' Gerry yelled, half annoyed, half laughing.

She grabbed my hand and started running back the way we'd come.

'What are you doing?' I said, my feet pounding on the earth as she pulled me along. Gerry had said she knew these boys, that they'd met at this resort every summer for years, that they were always trying it on with her. They must have had their own little games.

'Let them chase us,' she said, whispering

as she ran, her breath coming out in big white puffs of condensation.

I looked back over my shoulder as Gerry dragged me along. Jason and Nick were up and heading in our direction.

'Argh!' I screamed, really excited. 'Run faster!'

I imagined them catching up with us. Nick grabbing me, saying 'Gotcha!' and gently tackling me to the floor, both of us laughing. We might even kiss.

We ran as fast as we could. My heart was racing and my breath burned my throat, but the adrenalin filling my body pushed out all the fear. We laughed and laughed as we sprinted.

We got through the gate and back to the trees we rounded earlier, a lot closer to the sheer drop off the cliff. 'Careful,' I whispered, and slowed down. The path was less than a metre from the edge.

But Gerry didn't slow – she dropped my hand and ran way ahead of me. Suddenly I was scared again – if she abandoned me now, I was completely stranded, completely at the mercy of those boys I didn't know, who we had just really, really narked off.

A little way along, the cliff stopped being a sheer drop and sloped more gently towards its edge. Gerry turned her back to the sea and headed down towards the cliff face.

'What are you doing?' I screeched.

'Hide!' she said, still making her way down the cliff to where the grassy bit stopped and the rocky bit began.

I didn't want to, but I could hear the boys' heavy feet and their panting not far behind us. Besides, where else was I going to go? I took a deep breath and got down on my hands and knees, the wet grass instantly soaking through my leggings. It was slippery, and my imagination flashed images of me losing my grip, smashing my head against the rocks, the morning news with footage of my parents searching the sea for their missing child.

I backed down the slope as carefully as I could, turning to see where I was putting my feet.

The boys were getting closer.

'Hurry up,' said Gerry, giggling.

I got to the rock she was hiding behind and lay next to her, both of us panting but trying to do it as quietly as possible. We waited.

The boys ran past above us.

'If that was Liam and Joe,' one of them said, hacking a little – smokers' cough – 'I'm gonna kill them.'

Gerry covered her mouth to hide her laughter. I pressed my lips together.

'Little rats,' the other one said.

Their footsteps pounded away down the path. We didn't say anything, we didn't move at all, not until we couldn't hear them any more. Then Gerry started laughing.

'That was hilarious!' she whooped. 'You were so funny! You were so scared!'

'Scared?' I said. 'I was terrified! They looked so angry. What do you think they would have done if they caught us?'

'They probably would have been a bit grumpy, but a couple of kisses would have made up for it.'

'So why didn't we let them?!' I said. I'd

never kissed anyone before. The idea made me nervous, but this was all going to be part of the new me – New Abby. Cool Abby. The kind of girl that kissed boys she met on holiday.

'The thing is,' Gerry said, 'I didn't want to say anything, because I didn't want it to spoil our fun, but . . . well . . . I have a boyfriend.'

Oh. That sort of made sense, I suppose.

'His name is Mack, and we're totally in love.'

Now I was jealous. Like Tara, Gerry had got a boyfriend before I did.

'I love him,' she said, 'and he wouldn't like it if he knew I was hanging out with other boys.'

'Right,' I said. I tried not to be annoyed that she'd got my hopes up. 'So why did you arrange to meet up with them in the first place?'

Gerry sighed. 'I thought *you* wanted to. You said you liked Nick – the fa— the dark-haired one. So I didn't want to ruin it for you. But now I've ruined it anyway.' She pouted. 'You hate me now, don't you?' Her voice went deep and gravelly. 'You don't want to be my friend any more, do you?'

'Of course I want to be your friend!' I said.

The holiday would have been so rubbish without Gerry. 'But next time, let me in on the plan before we do it, OK?'

'OK!' she said, jumping up and pulling me up after her. I used my phone to light our way. We walked along in silence for a bit.

'Actually, there is this boy I really like at home,' I told her.

'Oooooh,' she said, and her eyes lit up, catching the light from my phone. 'Do tell.'

This was a first – someone listening to me talk about my crush. A rare occurrence when I was with Tara.

'Well, his name is Joel. He plays bass in Sucker Punch . . .'

The house was still dark when I climbed back in through my window. Looked like I'd got away with it. I gave Gerry a thumbs-up, and she waved at me before running off.

I scrambled out of my wet leggings and got into bed, still shivering in my lacy green top.

My head was buzzing. Gerry was a maniac. The night had been terrifying . . . but also awesome. It was the first time in ages I hadn't been worried about any of the things I normally worry about – my sister, schoolwork, stuff with boys at home. It felt amazing.

And it was all thanks to Gerry.

Upstairs I heard Becky call out for Mum. I listened to make sure she was OK. There was shuffling as Mum walked across the hall.

'Are you all right, darling?' she said anxiously as she opened her door.

'Can I have a drink, please, Mum?' Becky replied, her voice croaky.

And I relaxed.

That night had been exactly what I needed to take my mind off things. I deserved to spend a couple of hours not worrying about my sister.

I closed my eyes and smiled. I couldn't wait to tell Tara and the rest of the Boys' School Girls about it. I bet they wouldn't believe that Boring Flabby Abby had done anything so wild.

New Abby had taken over. And I was really starting to like her!

Chapter 5

I'm doodling on my homework diary. A little kitten dressed as a Christmas elf. Nothing else to do when Mrs Martin is taking the register.

'Now that's done,' she says, 'I want to remind you all about open day at the end of next week.'

I try to tune her out and draw long whiskers on the kitten.

'We really want to make a good impression on the prospective parents and students. So if you could try to keep the school – and yourselves – clean and tidy, that would be much appreciated.'

The kitten gets a Santa hat.

'And before you go off to class, I have an announcement to make.'

A big 'Ooooooh' comes from the class. I drop my pen and laugh with everyone else. Even Mrs Martin smiles. This must be a nice announcement. I look at Tara sitting next to me and we exchange excited eyebrow wiggles.

'This year there's going to be a Winter Festival up in Wimbledon Village . . .' she continues.

'Cool!' I say, and everyone starts whispering. Wimbledon Village is quite close to where me and Tara live and we go there all the time – it's a nice high street with loads of cafes and shops and things.

'It starts on the first Saturday of December, and on opening night they'll close the road to traffic and turn on the Christmas lights. There'll also be a firework display.'

Whoop! Whoop! If it's a schooly thing then Mum will definitely let me go.

'I wonder if they'll get a celeb to turn on the lights?' says Donna, sitting behind us.

'Maybe a footballer,' says Craig Hurst. 'Doesn't John Terry live around here?'

There is some booing from the boys who don't like John Terry for whatever reason.

'Katie Price does too,' says Donna.

That makes me and Tara boo like the boys just did, but some of them cheer. Typical.

'I'm sure there'll be a celebrity,' says Mrs Martin, rolling her eyes. 'But that's not really the point, is it? The school is going to have a stall there, with information about us, about how we are accepting female students, and we'll have a raffle . . .'

While Mrs Martin drones on about the school stuff Tara leans over and whispers, 'Maybe they'll want Sucker Punch to play at the festival.'

Somehow I doubt it.

'We could go in fancy dress,' I suggest. The kitten with the Santa hat is giving me an idea.

'Cool!' says Tara. 'Let's tell the others.'

As soon as the bell rings Obi, Candy, Hannah and Donna rush over to our desk. 'What do you reckon?' says Obi. 'Shall we go?'

'Definitely!' I say. Tara, Candy and Donna nod too.

'And Abby was just saying we could all get dressed up for it.'

If we could find a theme for every day of the year I would dress up for everything!

'Could be fun,' says Candy, twirling one of her blonde curls round her finger.

'What if no one else dresses up?' says Hannah. 'We might look really stupid.'

'And you know none of the boys will be bothered,' says Donna.

'Oh, so what?' I say. 'We don't have to do everything with boys you know.'

Donna frowns at me like I'm having a brain malfunction.

'I'll get Reece to join in,' says Tara. 'He'll persuade the other boys.'

Instantly I am slightly less enthusiastic.

'What was that, Abs?' Tara asks me.

I didn't mean to groan, but the girls act differently when the boys are around – it's like everything becomes a competition.

'Nothing,' I say.

'Come on,' Tara saying, leaning into me. 'We'll get Reece to get Joel to go too. Double date.'

That sounds cool . . . but this is the kind of thing I would normally do with just Tara. We never hang out just us two any more.

'Yeah, great,' I say.

'Come on, girls,' Mrs Martin comes over. 'Haven't you got classes to go to?'

I slowly start putting my stuff in my bag. I should stop being a misery guts; the festival will be fun. And the only way I'll get to go out with Joel is if we actually spend time together, right? Plus I need to start feeling happy for my friend.

'Hey, Tara!' Reece calls from the doorway. 'Sitting with me in maths?'

I freeze. Tara and I sit next to each other in everything. Whatever she says will prove if she still likes me as much, now she has a boyfriend.

'OK!' says Tara.

Traitor!

We made a promise when we started this school: mates over boys all the way. It seems that only applies to Tara when she wants it to.

'I might need you to help me with the answers,' Reece says, giving Tara a wink.

She beams at him and scurries to his side.

'Ahem,' Mrs Martin clears her throat. 'I hope that was a joke, Mr Lee.'

'Of course it was, Mrs Martin!' he says. 'I love maths . . . I mean, I'm only human!'

Mrs Martin mutters as she goes off to teach.

Reece and Tara have left and I have nothing to do except follow them to maths and hope I can find someone to sit next to. Trouble is, Sonia and Donna are the only other girls in our class, and they always sit next to each other. I'll have to sit by myself – or worse, next to Craig Hurst, the most horrible boy in the school.

I can't believe Tara's abandoned me so easily. But at least it makes me feel less guilty about the mean things I said about her.

It was pouring outside. Which hardly made a change from the usual weather in Wales. Gerry and I were sitting on my bed playing our seven-hundredth game of cards.

'Blackjack!' Gerry yelled.

'Aww! You cheat,' I said. Gerry had won almost every game.

'Did you call me a cheat?' she said, looking very serious.

'Joke!' I said, whacking her on the leg. 'I'm rubbish at cards.'

'Nah,' said Gerry, her face softening a little. 'I'm just lucky.' She shuffled backwards.

My foldaway bed wasn't very comfortable. She grabbed my pillow from behind her.

And there was my sketch pad. The page still open at the drawing of Tara.

'What's . . . ?' Gerry held up the pad.

I blushed and started gathering the cards together.

'Who's that?' she asked.

'Oh,' I said. 'That's my friend Tara.' I shrugged, trying not to be embarrassed. 'I was *really* bored so I—'

'It's good,' Gerry said. I appreciated her not making me feel stupid. 'She's pretty.'

'Yeah. But she's totally obsessed with her boyfriend Reece at the moment,' I say.

'Bleurgh,' said Gerry, sticking out her tongue. 'I had a friend like that. I mean, it's like, *So you've got a boyfriend. Doesn't mean you have to stop having a life!*'

'Exactly!' I say.

Gerry picked up the pad and took a pencil from the cardboard box I was using as a bedside table. 'Do you mind?'

I shrugged. 'Sure. It's only a doodle.' Even

though it *wasn't* only a doodle, I let her. I didn't want her to think I cared that much. New Abby didn't care about anything.

Gerry drew a massive speech bubble coming out of Tara's mouth. Inside the bubble she wrote:

Ooooooh, Reece. He's so dreamy!

I laughed. 'Give me the pencil.'

I scribbled '*Reece*' a few times around her head, to show how obsessed she was with him.

Gerry grabbed the pencil back. She blacked out one of Tara's teeth so it looked like it was missing. Suddenly it seemed too much.

'Hey!' I snapped.

Gerry paused and looked up at me. Her eyes grew wide like she was about to cry. It *was* too much, but I didn't want Gerry to think I hated her or anything, so I grinned. 'Give me that.' I took the pencil and drew a bogey coming out of Tara's nose. Then a big pair of glasses.

Gerry started laughing. 'Oooh, I'm Tara,' she said, putting on a high-pitched voice. 'I think I'm so special because a boy likes me.'

'That's good,' I say. 'You should put that.'

Gerry nods at the pencil in my hand. 'You do it.'

I write:

Oooh, I'm Tara. I can't think my own thoughts unless my boyfriend tells me to.

Gerry covered her mouth as she laughed.

I'm Tara. I'm so great.

I knew we were being mean. But it was just a bit of silliness. It wasn't like Tara would ever find out or anything.

At least, that's what I told myself.

Chapter 6

'Could I have Abigail, please, Mrs Bartlet?' The headmaster – Mr McAdam – has stuck his head around the door. Instantly, my stomach drops and my cheeks feel like they've been sucked in by a hoover. Everyone's looking at me. Somehow I manage to pack my bag, not making eye contact with anyone.

I walk to the front and Mr McAdam smiles at me in a way that lets me know this is going to be bad. As he closes the door behind us, I can just hear Tara say, 'Can I go with her, Mrs Bartlet?' and her chair scrape back.

Mr McAdam says, 'I'm afraid your sister . . .' and the world goes all watery. My sister's condition is worse and my dad is coming to pick me up. If this was the first time this had happened I'd be crying, but it's not the first time – it's, like, the millionth time – so I don't. The Becky Lump is lodged in my throat.

Tara takes my arm. I didn't even notice she was here. 'I'll wait with Abby, Mr McAdam.'

'Thank you, Tara,' he says. 'You're a good friend.'

I say nothing. I'm afraid of what will happen if I do.

Tara starts leading me towards the exit. 'Do you need your coat?' she asks.

I shake my head. I just hope I can get out before the bell goes for the end of the day.

There it is. Too late.

People start pouring out of classrooms. I feel like everyone's going to stare at me and Tara for being out here early – but another thing I've found since starting Hillcrest is that if a girl looks like she's about to cry, boys tend to keep their distance.

I'm halfway down the corridor when I hear, 'Hey!' from Obi.

When I turn around she's surrounded by all our friends. I guess girls sniff out tears like sharks sniff out blood.

'Don't you dare!' says Indiana, hands on hips.

I give a half-smile at their pretend anger.

'Donna texted and said you'd been pulled out of class,' says Hannah.

'You didn't think you could leave without getting a hug from us, did you?' says Maxie.

They rush forward together like a rugby scrum to give me a group hug. The Becky Lump grows and I press my lips together to keep from crying.

I start steering the whole group towards the main doors. My dad will be here any minute.

'And we're all going to come to the hospital with you – you know, cheer your sister up,' says Candy.

Tara throws me a look. She gets how awkward this is. As kind as the offer is, it's not very practical. Firstly, there's no way that the nurses would let them all in. Secondly, an onslaught of visitors would stress my sister out. She would appreciate them coming, but she would feel the need to entertain everyone, to be fun and happy and laugh at their jokes.

That's if she's even able to open her eyes or speak.

'Thanks. You're so sweet, but there won't be space in the car,' I tell them quickly.

The buzz leaves the girls and I feel like a spoilsport.

'Sorry,' I add.

'You have nothing to be sorry for,' says Tara, grabbing my hand. 'Just know that whenever Becky wants to see a mass of crazy girls, we'll be there.'

The rest of them giggle.

'Thanks again, guys.'

'And if she could time it to get us out of double maths, that would be brill,' says Sonia, and Donna thumps her on the arm.

We've reached the front gates, and the boys are streaming past us.

Reece comes over and puts his arm around Tara. I'm nudged aside a little because Tara's still holding my hand.

'Everything OK, Abby?' Reece asks.

I nod.

Joel and Lenny appear beside him. Normally

I would suck in my stomach but I'm too worried about Becky to care how I look.

'Hey, Abby,' Joel says, and his face is a weird scrunched-up frown. The best thing about Becky being ill is also the worst thing about Becky being ill – the sympathy makes me feel loved and pitied at the same time.

'Hi,' I say.

It's a bit awkward as he tries to think of something to say. Then he opens his arms and steps into me. He wraps me up and gives me a hug. Sometimes actions speak louder than words, and up against his chest, still holding Tara's hand, I smile.

'We were going to the hospital but Abby said she doesn't want us there,' says Donna.

'It's not that!' I say, even though she's right. She saw through my lie. 'It's just . . .'

Donna flaps her hand at me. 'Don't worry, Abby.' She turns and bats her eyelashes at Lenny and flips her hair. 'Who fancies a coffee?'

The others nod and start drifting off towards the shops, but Tara hasn't moved –

she's still got her fingers firmly locked in mine.

'You coming, Tara?' Maxie asks her. Maxie is her sister – just eleven months older than her, so we're all in the same year.

Tara shakes her head. 'I'll meet you there. I'm going to wait with Abby.'

Maxie nods. She gets it. She's known me almost as long as Tara has.

Reece kisses Tara's cheek, then walks off with the rest of them. All of them waving and shouting that they love me. Tara doesn't say a word.

I get my phone and post on Facebook that I'm off to the hospital. Tara's watching me. She gets her phone out and is the first to comment, sending me a kiss.

My dad's car appears, coming round the roundabout outside school. Even from here I can see his hardened, sad face. He wishes there was someone he could blame for all of this, someone he could be angry at. But there's no one, so he's angry at himself.

'There's your dad,' says Tara. 'I'll leave you

guys to it. But text as soon as you can to let me know how she is, yeah?' She gives me a hug for as long as it takes for my dad's car to pull up next to us. 'Love you loads, Abby.'

'Thanks, Tara,' I say. 'Love you too.'

Tara waves at my dad, pulling the saddest smile that's ever been smiled. Then she walks away.

With every step Tara takes I feel weaker. Like I'm an inflatable and she's pulling out the stopper. 'Actually, Tara,' I call out, 'could you come with us?'

She's back by my side in a second. 'Of course.'

'You don't mind not meeting up with Reece?'

She doesn't even bother to reply. She opens the door and gets into the car before I do.

'Hi, Mr Gardner,' she says. 'Is it OK if I come too?'

My dad smiles at her, much more widely than he does at me. 'Hello, Tara. Of course.'

I get in behind her. Tara holds my hand the whole way. I wish I hadn't doubted her earlier today. Yeah, she might ditch me in a maths class, but she's always there for me when I need her. That's what real friendship is about.

I look down at our joined hands and the *Best Friends Forever* bracelet I gave her. I wish I still had mine.

Chapter 7

We walk through the hospital, taking the back way so we don't have to go through A & E.

'Look at you,' says Tara, 'knowing all the sneaky routes.'

'Last time I went through A & E I saw someone throw up,' I tell her. 'Almost made *me* throw up. So Adrian showed me this way.'

Tara gasps and puts her hand to her heart. 'Will Adrian be here?' she whispers, even though I'm sure Dad isn't listening to us.

I nod. 'And he's even more swoon than ever,' I tell her. But it's just a joke. Adrian is one of the nurses who works on my sister's ward. I've known him for so long that he's more like a big brother than a crush.

When we arrive at the front desk of the ward, Adrian's there.

'Hello, ladies,' he says in his strong Irish accent. 'Looking lovely . . .'

'*As always*,' the three of us say together and laugh.

Dad doesn't join in. He gives the nurses a quick nod then goes straight over to the room where Becky is.

There's a new nurse standing next to Adrian, one I've only met once. She's tall and thin with hair scraped back tight, and I've never seen her smile. 'It's family only,' she says, scowling at Tara. 'Rebecca is very sick.'

Tara cringes and looks at me.

'It's OK,' Adrian says. 'Tara *is* family.'

I throw him a sneaky smile. I love that we're in it together.

The new nurse huffs and rolls her eyes. 'Fine,' she says, grabbing a clipboard and walking away.

No sympathy from her, then.

Tara peers into all the smaller rooms as we walk through the ward. She's putting a brave face on it, but she's nervous. She's been here quite a few times, but not nearly as often as I have.

There are worse things to see than someone vomiting. People crying is almost unbearable. Dads crying is the worst.

We get a little further and Becky's voice makes me and Tara smile at each other.

'. . . can't put a five on a nine!' she's saying. She sounds a little croaky but she's bossing someone around, which means she's acting normally. 'Pick up the pack!'

'And *you* can't keep changing the rules to suit yourself,' Mum says, forcing jolliness into her voice. 'That's called cheating.'

We enter a room on the left. There are four beds in here, but only one apart from Becky's is filled. The girl in that bed is asleep and pale and doesn't look like she'll be waking up any time soon. A woman – presumably her mum – is holding her hand, just staring at her. If she's anything like my mum, she'll do nothing but that for hours.

I walk straight past without batting an eyelid. Tara stares a little, then stops herself and turns to Becky. Becky has the bed nearest the window – the nicest one. It's one of the perks of all the nurses knowing her so well.

She's so tiny. She's only seven, and a *small* seven. Her legs don't reach even halfway down the bed and they look like little mouse burrows under the sheets.

'Tara!' she yells, when she finally looks up from her cards.

'Hey, sexy Bexy,' Tara says.

Becky grins, which makes Mum smile.

'Hello? Am I invisible?' I say to her.

Becky grins at me now, pushing the strands of thin blondish hair back from her face. She has a cannula in the back of her hand, with a tube that leads up to a drip. 'Hi, Abby,' she says. 'I *am* happy to see you, really.'

I roll my eyes at her, but she knows I'm only joking.

Mum comes over and gives me a hug. 'I'm happy to see you too,' she says, kissing me on the top of my head.

Mum looks terrible. In fact she looks more sick than Becky does. And her eyes are ringed red with huge bags underneath. There are beds in the hospital where parents can sleep, but Mum mostly stays here in the chair.

She sniffs. 'How was school?'

I stick my tongue out. 'School-y.'

Mum smiles a dead smile.

I don't know what's up with Becky, but I'm guessing the kidney infection she had when she left Wales has got worse. She gets them all the time, but when they're really bad she needs to be in hospital for the treatment.

'Nice handbag,' Tara says, pointing to the drip hanging above Becky's head. 'Where did you get it?'

Becky giggles. 'Gucci.'

'I want the same one,' says Tara. 'But maybe in purple.'

Becky giggles again.

Mum and Dad both look on with the same expression: a fixed, adoring smile, like they've been hypnotized.

Then Mum whispers that she'd like to speak to me. This is a bad *speak to me*, I can tell. 'While you and Tara trade fashion tips, your dad and

I are just going to be outside talking to your sister,' Mum tells Becky.

Becky ignores her — she's too engrossed in whatever game Tara's inventing.

There's a ringing that starts up in my ears, like a high-pitched dial tone. My legs go wobbly, but somehow we get out of the room. I look around for a place to sit, but all the wall space is taken up with different machines on wheels. We stand in a huddle in the middle of the corridor.

I clench my teeth, waiting.

'How are you?' Mum asks me. 'Everything all right at school?'

'Everything's fine with school,' I say, a little too snippy. I wish she'd get on with it.

'Good.'

'What's wrong with Becky?'

This is a stupid question — there are a million things wrong with Becky. When Becky was born they knew straight away she had problems. I was only six at the time, but I remember Mum and Dad going off to have the baby, and then my aunt Jenny and uncle Wes moving into our house as Mum and Dad had to be in hospital for ages. Becky was in special care.

Ever since, she's been in and out of hospital for one problem or another. One of her kidneys doesn't work very well. The other doesn't work at all, so she's always getting sick with infections that last longer and hit harder than they would for most people. She can't walk very well either, not over long distances, so she needs a wheelchair. When she gets sick, Mum and Dad call Dr Hayward – her consultant – and she winds up straight back here.

Mum and Dad exchange a glance before looking back at me. 'She's pretty bad this time,' Mum says.

There it is. The world drops and my knees go. I steady myself and face my mum, trying to act mature.

'She's stable at the moment, and she's doing OK . . .' Mum shudders back a breath, 'for now.'

Dad grabs Mum's hand. It's his turn to take over. 'Dr Hayward says the only way to fix it is if Becky gets a new kidney.'

Becky's been on the transplant list for years. It's really horrible that we're waiting for someone to die so that my sister can get her life back.

'And if she doesn't?' I ask.

'She's going to carry on like this for the rest of her life . . .' says Mum. 'Dialysis all the time. In and out of hospital with serious infections . . . until . . .'

There's an end to this sentence that she doesn't say. '*One of the infections kills her . . .*'

Becky's been on the waiting list for a long time. Hopefully a suitable donor will become available one of these days. But if not, sooner or later, without that kidney, my little sister is going to die.

Chapter 8

The Becky Lump is so big right now that it's almost blocking my windpipe. I'm finding it hard to breathe. Becky needs a kidney. As soon as possible. Before she gets hit with an illness she's too weak to fight off.

Mum and Dad both told the doctors they would give up their kidneys, but when they got tested Dad wasn't compatible and Mum has a couple of health issues so they wouldn't let her — no matter how much she begged.

'I want to—' I start, but Mum and Dad rush at me and both of them hug me tight.

'No, darling!' Mum says, a tear coming from the corner of her eye and streaking down her face.

'But it could—' I say.

Even Dad's voice catches as he speaks. 'We know that. And your mother and I have talked a lot about it,' he says. 'We've decided we're not willing to put you through it.'

I have two healthy kidneys and only need one. Becky has none. But my parents still won't let me give her one of mine.

My first reaction is relief, which makes me feel like an awful person. But my second reaction is fear – I don't want to lose my sister. 'But—' I try again.

'We're not having this conversation again,' says Mum. 'We're not willing to put you through a serious operation. Not at your age. Although it's very brave of you to offer.'

We all go silent. I'm thinking about what this means, for Becky, for my parents, for me.

'So how long until they find a kidney?' I ask.

Dad looks angry – again blaming himself for not being able to get his daughter the one thing she needs. The right kidney could come along today . . . or it could take years. In the end, it just comes down to luck. What if it doesn't come in time?

Dad pulls me close. 'We're going to get

through this, Abigail,' he says, clearly reading my mind. 'Don't you worry. She'll be fine.'

But the way he says it makes me worry more. I know he has no idea if she'll be fine or not. And Mum starts to cry so Dad leaves me and puts his arm around her. When I see them hugging like that I realize that the two of them have their own personal horror film they're living through, and it's a million times worse than my life.

Mum dabs her face with a tissue and we all go back into the room, where Becky and Tara are still chatting away.

I push the Becky Lump down by gulping hard and say, 'What have you two been gossiping about?'

Becky taps her nose. 'Secret,' she says.

'I've been telling Becky about school, and all the hunky boys.'

Becky's eyes are wide. 'It sounds amazing.'

'Oh dear,' says Dad. 'Tara, Becky's only seven. She's not interested in boys yet – please, God.'

We all have a little laugh. 'Poor Dad,

surrounded by women all the time,' I say. 'Now you know what it's like for me being surrounded by boys at school.'

'Speaking of school,' Dad says, looking at his watch. 'Hadn't I better get Tara home?'

Tara doesn't move; she just looks at me. She'll do whatever I tell her. Yet another reason why she's my best friend and I should have never doubted it.

'Go on,' I say to her. 'I'll see you tomorrow.'

Tara picks up her bag and comes over to hug me. I squeeze her tight so her voice comes out a bit squashed. 'Give me a call later, OK?'

'Mum,' I say, 'why don't you go too? Get out of the hospital for a bit.'

Mum starts shaking her head so I continue: 'Go on. You can stop by the house and have a shower. Get yourself some more stuff.'

Dad squeezes her hand. 'Come on, love. Come home with me for a bit.'

'I'll be here with Becky,' I say.

'Yeah,' says Becky. 'Abby has to tell me her secrets too.'

Mum is finally convinced and she gives me and Becky a kiss. The kiss she gives Becky is much longer than the kiss she gives me – like she's not sure when she's going to see her again. 'I'll be less than two hours, OK?'

Becky nods.

I shuffle the chair so I'm even closer to Becky and we watch as Mum and Dad each put an arm around Tara's shoulders and they leave.

'Thanks so much, Tara,' Mum's saying to her as they walk out. 'Becky loves seeing you. And we're so grateful Abby has such a wonderful friend . . .'

'So . . . what's new with you?' Becky asks. 'Now the rents have gone, you can tell me everything.'

I tell her about the Winter Festival in the village.

'I hope I'm out of here by then,' she says, then yawns. 'Do you think Mum and Dad will let me go?'

'I don't see why not,' I say. 'If you're well enough.'

She yawns again. He eyes have glazed a little

and the dark bags – just like Mum's – have suddenly appeared.

'You go to sleep,' I tell her. 'I'll stay here.'

I'm about to grab my bag for my book but Becky says, 'Carry on talking. Please.' She closes her eyes. 'I'll go to sleep, but you carry on talking.'

This is a thing Becky has wanted since she was a baby. She doesn't like to go to sleep in case we're not there when she wakes up. We have to talk while she drifts off.

'The girls and I were thinking of getting dressed up,' I start, changing my voice to a whisper. Becky settles down and her breathing starts to change. 'I want to look pretty, but I want to look Christmassy too.' Becky's already asleep, I can tell, but I carry on talking – it's quite soothing for me too. 'Maybe me and Tara could—'

'I'll go with you.'

I nearly jump out of my skin. When I see who it is I *do* jump out of my skin. Well, out of my chair at least.

'Gerry!'

Her auburn hair looks so pretty now that it's not being blown all over the place by the Welsh wind. And she's paler. Her face was always so rosy when I saw her in the countryside – I guess because of the weather. She's wearing blue tracksuit bottoms and a tight Roxy T-shirt, just like the one I have. I remember her admiring it on holiday. She must have got herself one.

For a second I wonder if I've fallen asleep too, and if Gerry is a dream. But she runs towards me, her bouncy curls bobbing up and down, she wraps me in a giant hug and I know it's real.

'Gerry! I can't—'

She puts her finger on her lips and gestures to Becky sleeping. Becky hasn't moved but I lower my voice anyway.

'I can't believe you're here!' I say. 'How did you get here? How did you even know where I was?'

Gerry takes out her brand-new smartphone. 'The wonders of Facebook,' she says.

Of course, I posted that I was coming. There are twelve comments – the Boys' School Girls sending their love.

'How did you get past Nurse Nasty?' I ask her.

'She gave me the third degree, asking loads of questions and saying no one can come in unless they're related,' says Gerry. 'But I told her I was your cousin.'

I have to laugh. 'You're brilliant.'

'It's not *that* brilliant. I saw you were coming to the hospital so I got straight on the tube and came over.'

'You came all the way from Barnet? That's *miles*!'

Gerry shrugs. 'Just a tube and two bus rides,' she says.

I'm totally blown away that she would make all this effort for me. 'Wow,' I say. 'Thank you so much.'

'What are best friends for?'

I gulp, and glance over to Becky to see if she heard that. I grin at Gerry again, ignoring what she just said.

'How is she?' she asks. 'Has she been in hospital since the holiday?'

The flashback of the ambulance leaving the

cottage races through my mind. I nod. 'Today she got worse,' I say. 'The doctor said she needs a new kidney as soon as possible. Becky's tough, but she can't go on like this forever.'

'Of course she can't.' Gerry tips her head to the side.

'We wouldn't mind the waiting, if we just knew when it was going to have a happy ending.'

Gerry puts a hand on my arm, sympathetic, then changes the subject. 'Hey. Who was that girl I saw your parents leaving with?'

'Tara,' I tell her.

'The girl in the picture you drew? The one who was so obsessed with her boyfriend she'd been ignoring you?'

I nod, feeling guilty about saying all that mean stuff about Tara when she's been so brilliant today. 'Tara's pretty cool really.'

'Oh,' says Gerry, her face darkening a little.

Have I said something to upset her? 'Why do you ask?'

'I thought it was you at first,' says Gerry, 'because your mum and dad had their arms around her. I ran up to them, thinking it was you, but your parents obviously didn't remember me.' She looks hurt and the clouds on her face are back again.

'Don't take it personally,' I say, trying to reassure her. 'They only met you that one night.'

'Oh, I'm not offended,' Gerry says quickly, plastering on a smile that isn't quite real. 'But I did look like an idiot waving and yelling. So I pretended it was at someone behind them and ran right past.'

I explode with a laugh, then cover my mouth as I remember Becky asleep. 'I wish I'd seen that.' I'd forgotten how easy it was to laugh when I was with Gerry. She's made me laugh at times when I thought I'd never laugh again.

Gerry raises her eyebrows at me. 'Not funny.' She smirks.

'Quite funny.'

We both turn to Becky, but she hasn't moved. Even after my outburst.

'I wish I had a sister,' says Gerry.

I hang my head. 'It's harder than you think sometimes.'

Gerry pulls her mouth to one side. 'Of

course it is, sorry.' She does look sorry for what she said, but there is something else too. She seems so lonely that she's become jealous . . . of *me*. Why anyone would want to be like me is a mystery. Boring Flabby Abby and her sick sister. But Gerry sees something in me that other people don't. And it's really nice to be around that for a change.

'It's OK.' I reach over to her. 'I have brilliant friends.'

I think of the way the girls waved me off from school − all totally ready to come to hospital with me. I think of the way they've all commented on Facebook, sending me so much love. I think of the way Gerry has travelled across London to see me.

'Like Tara?' she asks slowly.

'Yeah. Tara and I have been friends since the first day of primary.'

'Of course,' she says. 'But she's not your *best* friend, is she?' She squints as she looks at me intensely, then grabs my arm. She squeezes so tight it hurts. '*I'm* your *best* friend.'

'Umm . . .' I pull my arm out of her grip.

Now's the part where I have to tell her the truth; that Tara is my oldest and bestest friend in the world. My best friend forever. Nothing will ever beat that.

Gerry waves her wrist in the air. 'I have the friendship bracelet to prove it.'

The bracelet is pink and purple, with a silver disc on it saying '*Best Friends*'. And it's the one Tara gave to me. My heart sinks with guilt.

Gerry's being really full-on and I really can't deal with it right now.

How on earth am I going to get my bracelet back from Gerry? And why on earth did I give it to her in the first place?

Chapter 9

I'd pressed myself against the wall of the stairs to let the paramedics past. But the holiday cottage was tiny and there wasn't enough space for them to get by.

'Abby! Move!' Dad shouted.

It hurt that he yelled. I was only standing there because I'd been going to shut the door the ambulance people left open.

'Sorry,' I said, and jumped down the stairs, tucking into the small room at the side that doubled as my bedroom.

I watched from the doorway. The two paramedics were holding either end of the stretcher, keeping Becky straight as they carried her down. Mum and Dad stood watching from the top landing, Dad making fists with his hands. Mum's shoulders were so tense they were practically up at her ears.

'Mummy,' Becky whimpered, and reached out. Becky never whimpered; she was normally so strong.

'I'm here, darling,' Mum said, following. 'I'm right behind you.'

My aunt puts her hand on my shoulder, making me jump. She didn't say anything. There were tears in her eyes.

My baby sister – so small. Taken to hospital again. It had happened a lot, but never in the middle of the night by ambulance like that. Never an emergency.

'Are they taking me all the way to London?' Becky's little voice rose up from the stretcher. I couldn't see her face.

'Yes,' Mum replied. 'And your father and I will be right with you.' Mum wasn't really saying this to Becky, she was saying it to the ambulance men, daring them to contradict her.

'Abby?' said Becky.

'She'll stay here with Jenny and Wes,' Mum replied.

I couldn't see Becky's face and suddenly I got this huge feeling it was very important that

I did. I followed them outside to the waiting ambulance.

The blue lights were so bright in the darkness of the Welsh countryside. A few people came out of their houses, all in their pyjamas, being nosey but pretending to care.

I squeezed past the paramedic before he could lift her in. He gave me a look, then saw it was me and softened.

'Bye, Bex,' I said to her. I picked up the bunny that was lying beside her on her stretcher. 'Look after Bunny, OK? You know he gets travel-sick.'

Becky did her best to smile.

'Sorry, pet.' The ambulance man nudged me out the way to take his place. 'We've got to go.'

They hauled her inside the van.

'Abby! Abby!' I turned to see a mass of ginger hair racing towards me. She smashed into me, grabbing me for a hug. 'Are you OK?' she said.

'My sister,' I said, pointing to the ambulance, figuring it was all the explanation needed.

Gerry looked at the ambulance and shook her head. 'Oh God. That's terrible.'

Mum came over to me, her leather overnight bag in her hand.

'Mum, this is my friend Gerry. The girl I've been telling you about?'

Mum barely glanced at Gerry. She gave only a half-smile, then looked back at me. 'Will you be OK?'

I nodded. 'Of course.' I always was.

'It'll take a few hours, but we'll call when we get to the hospital to let you know we've arrived,' Mum said, 'and again in the morning. Don't stay awake to hear from us though. They'll wake you if there's any news. Won't you, Jen?'

Auntie Jenny was right by Mum's side. 'Of course I will.'

'You go back to sleep, and enjoy the rest of your holiday,' Mum said. 'You deserve it.'

While Mum and my aunt hugged, Dad stepped forward. 'We'll see you at the end of the week, sweetheart,' he said to me, giving me a kiss. 'And sorry that I shouted at you just now.'

'It's OK, Dad,' I said, swallowing past the Becky Lump.

'You're a good girl, you know that?' He patted my arm.

They waved goodbye. Dad got into the ambulance first and helped Mum in after him. 'Come on, old lady,' he said to her, but no one laughed.

My aunt had her arm round me, and Gerry came to the other side and held my hand. We watched the ambulance drive off into the darkness. The neighbours who'd come to gawp finally sloped off. One called out for us to let them know if they could be any help. They meant well, but what could they do? We didn't know these people. Everyone was just there on holiday. We'd never see each other again.

My aunt turned back to the cottage, guiding me with her. She flinched in surprise when she found Gerry on the end of my other arm. 'Sorry,' she said. 'Didn't see you there.'

'I'm Gerry. I'm Abby's friend.'

Auntie Jenny smiled at her like she'd just solved a puzzle. 'So *that's* where Abby's been running off to all day every day,' she said. 'You've put a smile on her face while she's been here.'

Gerry beamed. 'She's put a smile on mine!'
She was sucking up.

'Why don't you two come in and I'll make some hot chocolate?' she said, steering us both inside, still hand in hand. 'Then we can all walk Gerry back home. Where are you staying, Gerry?'

'In the hotel complex at the top of the hill,' she said. 'You don't need to walk me back. It's not far.'

'But it is very late.' Jenny looked at her watch as if to make a point. It was after midnight and I wondered if Gerry's parents had any idea that she was with me, or if she sneaked out every night, like she had made me do on her birthday.

'I'd love a hot chocolate,' I told Jenny, 'thank you. But can we drink it out here?' It was cold, but I couldn't feel it. And just the thought of going inside felt kind of claustrophobic. 'Pleeeeeease, Jenny?'

Pleeeeeease, Jenny was a thing we always did. I whined and Jenny always gave in. As long as I didn't push it too far I could have whatever I wanted.

'OK,' she said, 'you two sit here and I'll bring them out. And I'll bring you a coat too.' She looked at Gerry. 'And then I insist that we walk you home.'

I sat down on the little bench on the porch and sighed.

As Gerry sat, she muttered something under her breath: the word 'nightmare' and another word much ruder than that.

I was shocked at her swearing. But then I burst out laughing – it was possibly the most brilliant thing anyone had ever said about all this.

'What?' she said, looking completely confused.

'Nothing,' I replied. 'It's just that you've hit the nail right on the head.'

Gerry started laughing too.

'You're the best, Gerry,' I told her.

She stopped laughing. 'Do you really think so?'

'Yup. Definitely. Thank you so much,' I said. She must have seen the ambulance arrive and run straight down here to see what was wrong.

I'd only known her four days, but she'd become a really good friend. She always listened to me. She thought I was cool. She brought out a side of me I didn't even know was there. I'd never found it when I was with Tara.

Auntie Jenny brought us the hot chocolate and two massive coats that must have belonged to her and Uncle Wes. And then she left us to it.

'Can I tell you something I haven't told anyone?' I said.

Gerry's blue eyes were twinkling in the light from the house. 'Of course.'

'I'm going to give my sister my kidney.'

Gerry gasped. 'Really?'

'I think so.' I'd thought about it loads but that was the first time I'd said it out loud. I'd never even mentioned it to Tara.

We'd known for a while that a new kidney would help Becky's situation, but it was only recently that I realized I might actually be able to give her one of mine. 'My parents haven't asked me to do it – they don't expect it of me. I guess there must be loads of risks involved.'

'Could you die if you gave her your kidney?' Gerry asked.

I bit down on my lip. 'These operations are always risky, you know. But they know what they're doing. I hope!' My attempt at a joke.

'I couldn't stand it if you died!' she wailed, a little too dramatically. I saw tears in her eyes. 'I think I would die too.'

Sweet of her, but a little over the top. She'd only known me a few days.

'I've looked it up,' I told her, 'and the main thing about living with one kidney is that you have to take good care of yourself; drink loads of water and eat healthily all the time. Not too many sweets.'

Gerry stuck her tongue out. 'That's no fun,' she said.

It was true. I love junk food. 'But it's my *sister*,' I said. 'I have to, don't I?'

Gerry didn't say anything, she just stared out into the distance. There were the tall cliffs where we were chased by the boys the other night. The sea below. The moon shining above. You could just make out a row of tents on the field, and a couple of sheep that had wandered away from the herd.

'I've never met anyone like you,' Gerry said. 'You're really brave, Abby.'

'People are always saying I'm brave. But all I've had to do is be normal while my sister's sick. Giving up a kidney would be a brave thing to do. I'd like to live up to the title.'

'And you know I'll be there for you,' Gerry said, putting her hand over mine. 'If you decide to do this, I'll come and visit you in hospital. Every day. I'll wipe your chin if you're dribbling.'

I laughed. 'Hey!'

Gerry laughed too. 'I mean it,' she said.

But she didn't really mean it. Not really. We'd got close over the last few days because we were the only two twelve-year-olds in the area. At the end of half-term, she would go back home to her life and I would go back to mine. She'd be too busy to meet up with me.

'I'll be there for you every step of the way,' she continued. 'Because you're my best friend.'

It was a sweet thing for her to say, but it

made me feel a bit . . . awkward. Surely she must have a real best friend back home?

'Am I *your* best friend?' she asked.

I looked down into my cup, not quite willing to tell her the truth. I already had a best friend – a best friend forever. Tara and I had been inseparable since day one. But Gerry was being so nice, and I couldn't be rude.

'Hmm,' I said, with a vaguely positive nod.

Gerry pursed her lips together and it seemed like she was holding her breath. 'I can't believe it,' she said, as if I had just told her the cutest boy in our school fancied her. 'Really?'

I nodded. It was just a little white lie. It wouldn't hurt anyone.

'Who would have thought I'd make a best friend like you on holiday? You're so cool. And so nice. And you have such a big heart.'

Talk about full-on! But I supposed she was just being nice.

'Thanks, Gerry,' I said. 'You're pretty great yourself.'

Gerry fiddled with something around her wrist, then grabbed my arm. 'Here,' she said, pulling back the sleeve of my coat and pyjama top and tying a string round. 'I made you this. I was going to give it to you before you left but I want you to have it now. It's a friendship bracelet.'

'Thanks!' I said. She'd obviously made it herself and it wasn't very good. The colours were orange, blue and red – they didn't really go – and it was just done with a simple plait. But it was the thought that counted. 'That's so nice of you.'

Then she continued to fiddle with my wrist. My heart sank as I realized what she was doing.

'Er . . .' She was undoing the friendship bracelet Tara had given me. 'Gerry, you can't—'

'This is what best friends do,' Gerry said, 'swap bracelets. Now everyone will know we're BFFs forever.' She'd taken the bracelet and was already putting it on her own wrist.

'The thing is, Ger—' I started to say.

'D'oh!' she interrupted me, whacking herself on the forehead. 'You can't be BFFs *forever*,' she laughed. 'Then you'd be Best Friends Forever Forever! Ha!'

She jumped up and danced around on the spot. She seemed so happy that she'd gone a little manic.

'That hot chocolate kicking in?' I asked.

'Ha! Yeah! Sugar rush!' she said. 'I'll get going now.' She turned and skipped down the pathway.

'Wait!' I called.

I was about to tell her that I needed the bracelet back. That Tara had given it to me and she couldn't have it. But she was smiling so happily and I didn't want to upset her. I couldn't deal with that tonight. I would have to get it back tomorrow.

She was looking at me expectantly so I said, 'My aunt said we'd walk you.'

Gerry waved her hand at me. 'What's going to happen? I'm going to get attacked by a grumpy badger?' She was grinning and it made me grin too. 'I'll be fine. Save your aunt the hassle. Last thing she needs tonight.'

She bounded back and hugged me. 'Call me first thing in the morning. As soon as you know how your sister is doing.'

'I will,' I said, watching her dance off down the street.

'Bye, bestie!' she shouted as she skipped away.

If I couldn't get the bracelet back, I'd have to lie my way out of it. My little white lie had got a little out of control, and I'd only told it two seconds ago. Tara and I promised we'd *never* lie to each other, but Tara wouldn't forgive me if she knew I'd given her friendship bracelet away. How was I going to explain this to her?

But Tara would never find out, as long as she and Gerry never actually met.

I'd just have to make sure they never did.

Chapter 10

We're all giggling as we huddle into our meeting room — a little space inside the girls' loos where we know the boys can't listen in. We don't come in here every break time, not like we used to, but only for really important occasions — apparently, according to Donna, this is one of them.

'This place is beginning to smell more like a toilet now,' moans Hannah.

'It's fine!' says Tara bravely, but Hannah has a point. When we started here, the girls' toilets were brand-new — after all, this had always been a boys' school — and now there's a definite whiff of gross.

'So what's this all about, Donna?' Maxie asks. 'Why have you called us all here present?'

Me and Obi giggle. We love it when our meetings get pretend-serious.

Donna stands up on the big pipe that runs

along the wall and clears her throat to make us all shut up. 'Winter's a-coming, ladies,' she says. 'The Christmas event is coming to Wimbledon Village, and we have an emergency on our hands.'

I look at Tara to see if she has a clue what Donna's talking about. Tara shrugs at me. And from the look of the other girls, they have no idea either.

Donna rolls her eyes, clearly unimpressed. 'Girls! We haven't sorted out our outfits!'

Tara and I laugh, but Sonia, who would believe chipping her nail varnish was an emergency if Donna told her it was, starts to panic. 'Oh my God!' she says. 'How could we be so stupid?!'

I hear a message beep on my phone so I pull my bag off my back and get it out.

'Who is it?' asks Tara. The rest of them are focused on Donna.

'We need to make sure our outfits are, a) really clever, and b) really cool,' she's announcing.

I check the screen. It's not a message, but an Instagram alert. I have a new follower!

'We're the only girls in a school full of boys

and we don't want to let Hillcrest down, do we?'

'No!' says Sonia.

'Do we?' Donna says again, like this is panto or something.

'No!' all the girls shout together.

I only have sixty-eight followers on Instagram, even though I follow, like, more than five hundred people. A new follower doesn't happen every day. But I bet I know who it is. I let out a little squeak of excitement.

'What's the message?' asks Tara again.

But when I get to Instagram I see it:

Gerry Barnes.
@AbbysBFF

Why did she have to put *that* as her handle?

'Oooh,' says Candy, looking over my shoulder. 'Who's following you?'

'No one,' I say. I can't let Tara see this so I press my phone to my chest. 'It's nothing.' I can feel myself going red. 'Just a bookshop I follow following me back.'

'Which bookshop?' says Tara. 'If they follow back, I'll follow them. It's been ages since I got a new follower.'

'Umm . . .'

Tara and Candy are looking at me expectantly. I need to come up with a bookshop that definitely follows back.

'*Do* we?!' Donna shouts at us.

We have no idea what she's talking about, but Tara, Candy and me share a mock-cringe and shout, 'No!' at the top of our voices.

Donna scowls at us. 'So you *don't* want to look cool in front of everyone?'

I giggle.

'Er . . . no?' says Tara. And we all laugh.

'Sorry, Donna,' I say. 'We're listening now.'

'So we should get together regularly to discuss what we're going to go as . . .'

I get another alert on my phone. My first post from Gerry.

I'm now on Instagram because @Abbracadabra told me to. What's going on on here?

Getting a mention is my favourite thing in the world. I'm about to message back but when I look up everyone is watching me.

'Sorry,' I say.

Tara nudges me. 'What is it?' she says, motioning to my phone.

'Nothing,' I say again, but this time Tara's not buying it. She frowns at me. 'I'll tell you later,' I say. By then, hopefully I'll have worked out a way to explain everything and make it all OK. Maybe I can ask Gerry to change her username. Would that mean she'd have to get a new account? I don't want to hurt Gerry, but I have to tell her the truth. And I can't let Tara see this until I do.

What a mess!

'Donna,' says Hannah. She's actually put her hand up.

Donna tries to hide how pleased she is about this. 'Yes, Hannah?'

'What if we can't think of a good idea?' she says.

'Think harder,' Donna says. Which isn't very helpful.

'Abby's great at coming up with ideas,' says Tara.

I give Tara a nudge. 'You're pretty good too,' I say back.

'Get a room, you two,' Tara's sister Maxie jokes. She knows how close we are.

Tara and I stick out our tongues at her.

'In fact—' Tara starts, but my phone beeps again.

Donna rolls her eyes. 'Now I see why the teachers make us turn our phones off. Would you mind?' she says.

Everyone's looking at me as I check my phone.

Helloooo @Abbracadabra!
are you there @Abbracadabra?!

I quickly switch my phone to vibrate. Gerry can't expect an instant response.

'I had a good idea,' I tell them.

'Told you she would,' Tara says.

'How about we go as Santa's Little Helpers?'

'Oooh . . .' Everyone's interested.

'I saw these masks in a shop the other day,' I tell them. 'They have these cute pointy elf ears . . .' My phone is buzzing in my pocket. I stop talking to quickly check.

Does anyone know if @Abbracadabra follows back?
Hope so. She is my BEST friend after all lol

Another mention! Gerry's coming across as a little desperate.

'Nice,' says Obi.

'Or we could make our own,' Maxie says. 'That way they'll all be similar, but we can make them individual.'

Hannah groans. 'I am no good at things like that,' she says. 'Mine will be rubbish.'

'I'll help you,' I say. In my head I am already trying to visualize my own mask. I think I'll make it a half mask, only covering my eyes. Pointy ears at the side, with earrings in them too.

'Abby can help us all,' says Tara.

'I can,' I say. 'It'll be my very own Ask Abby.'

My phone buzzes again.

'You know we can still hear that, don't you?' says Donna. 'It's really distracting.'

'Sorry,' I say. I pull out my phone and this time I am going to turn it off. I have three new notifications – all from Gerry. *Give me a minute, won't you, Gerry?*

'Yeah,' says Candy. 'Who is it anyway?'

'There's no way a bookshop is super spamming you like that,' says Sonia, her eyes narrowing.

I'm bright red now. I have to think of something. Do I tell them all the truth – that it's my new friend Gerry and she's really nice? But then they'll see that she's calling herself my *best* friend.

My phone buzzes again.

'Oh, *come on!*' says Donna.

This time it's a text.

Haven't you seen my messages?
Why are you ignoring me?!!!

Wow. Now that's *definitely* desperate. It's a school

day so she should know that I might not be able to reply straight away.

I can't let the girls see this text or else they'll realize I lied when I said it was a bookshop before. 'Sorry, I'll turn it off.' I hold down the *Off* button but it doesn't shut down in time before Donna grabs my phone.

'Have you got a secret boyfriend or something?' she asks.

I try to grab the phone back. The girls start to giggle. I hope it's not at the idea that *I* could have a boyfriend.

'Why would I keep a boyfriend secret? It's just—' I say, still reaching for my phone.

Donna's shielded by Maxie and Sonia as she looks at my text.

'Who's Gerry?' she asks.

I'm glad it's only the text she's seen and not Gerry's handle.

'*Have* you got a secret boyfriend?' Sonia asks, eyes gigantic with disbelief.

Everyone is looking at me, waiting for me to respond. Why am I making such a big deal out of this? 'Gerry . . .'

'Gerry?' Tara asks. 'The girl from your holiday?'

'Yes,' I say. 'Now can I have my phone back?'

Donna looks at the screen. 'She wants to meet up with you,' she says. 'She's suggested Covent Garden this weekend.'

'Covent Garden is awesome!' says Indiana. 'They always have cool street performers there.'

'We should all go,' says Obi.

'We could get stuff to make our masks – get our outfits too,' Donna says.

Maxie pulls a face. 'Tara and I can't this weekend,' she says. 'We're at our dad's.'

But everyone else is too excited to listen to Maxie.

'Do you think Gerry will mind if we come too?' asks Indiana.

'Well, she is pretty cool.' I have everyone's full attention. No one ever really gives me attention, and now all eyes are on me. 'She's the most popular girl in her year at her school.' It's like Gerry's popularity is rubbing off on me.

'Really? How did you meet?' asks Maxie.

'Half-term. It started out as this lame holiday

in Wales, but then I met her. We even snuck out in the middle of the night to meet some boys.'

'Oh my God!' says Indiana.

'Really?' says Sonia.

'You never told me that,' says Tara.

'I only remembered it just now,' I say. I'm not sure why I didn't tell Tara. Maybe because of the friendship-bracelet thing. But maybe because I didn't think Tara would recognize the girl who climbed out the window in the middle of the night to meet strange boys on a cliff-top. I don't recognize her myself.

Donna is sneering. 'Are you sure this happened, Abby? Sure you didn't just imagine it?'

Sonia laughs behind her hand.

'Of course I'm sure!' I say. It might not sound like something I'd do, but I definitely did it. That week was the wildest I've ever been and I'm not letting Donna take it away from me. 'Gerry's so much fun. She has a really fit boyfriend called Mack. I've seen pictures of him.'

'Tell her to bring him this weekend,' says Hannah. 'And see if he has any friends he can bring along too.'

'Yeah!' says Indiana.

'Go on,' says Donna, 'ask her.' She shoves my phone in my face.

It would be really fun to hang out in central London and go shopping and stuff with Gerry. And I *would* like to meet Gerry's boyfriend, see if he's as nice as she says. But what if Tara sees Gerry wearing the friendship bracelet?

'Go on, Abby,' says Tara. 'I'd like to meet her.'

I can't.

'Just make it the weekend after next so me and Maxie can come too,' Tara adds.

And there's my out. I text Gerry.

Sorry I missed your messages — awesome you're on Instagram! I'd love to hang out in London. All my mates want to come too to meet you and your bf. Is that OK?

The reply comes straight away:

Yeahhhhh! I can't wait for my BFF to meet my BF. We're on.

'We're on,' I say to the girls.

The girls give a whoop. They all start talking at once, about how they've been to Covent Garden before, or how they haven't been up to town for ages.

'A proper girls' day out,' says Candy. 'Nice work, Abby.'

They're all looking at me like I'm so cool. Maybe a little of New Abby made it down from Wales after all.

'For the weekend after next though, yeah?' asks Tara.

I wince. 'Sorry, Tara,' I say. 'And Maxie – Gerry could only make this weekend.'

Tara looks at the floor. 'Fair enough,' she says.

I feel really guilty about cutting Tara out. But it's nice to be the centre of attention for once.

I'll just have this one fun weekend with Gerry, soak up the attention, then I'll stop seeing her. As long as Tara never notices Gerry's handle, or asks about the bracelet, it'll all be fine.

Chapter 11

'What do you think?' she says. 'Is it me?'

I turn around, expecting to see Gerry holding up another really cool T-shirt of some sixties band I've never heard of, but she's wearing a green curly wig. It clashes with the purple jeans she's wearing. The jeans are identical to the ones I have. I wore them a lot in Wales. I wonder if she bought them after she saw mine, or if it's just coincidence and she already had a pair.

The girls laugh. Candy is almost bent double from giggling.

Donna comes out in a pink tutu over her leggings. 'What about me?' she says. 'How stupid do I look?'

Actually, the tutu over leggings thing looks really cute. 'You look great!' I say to her. 'Are you going to buy it? If you don't, I will.'

Donna skips over to me. 'Do you think it's

nice, Abby? Really?' she asks. 'I'll buy it if you do – we could look the same.'

Donna usually hates it when people have the same outfit as her. Now she wants us to match! This is awesome.

And I have a feeling it's all down to one person.

'Gerry!' Donna calls. 'What do you think of my tutu? Abby and I are going to get one.'

Gerry swishes the wig from her head and comes over.

'I think it's ace! What other colours does it come in?'

'Why?' Donna asks, biting her lip. 'Do you not like this colour?'

Gerry starts pulling more tutus from a high shelf, making a complete mess as they come tumbling down. 'It's perfect for you,' she says, 'but I can't pull off that shade of pink with my ginger hair now, can I?' She starts holding up different coloured tutus and looking in the mirror.

Donna smiles like a little girl. 'So you're going to get one too?'

'Definitely!'

'Ace!' says Donna. Totally copying Gerry's word. Then she puts another pink tutu next to Gerry. 'And I don't know what you're talking about; you can totally pull off pink!' she says. 'Your hair is more auburn. It's not ginger like Sonia's.'

Sonia gives a shaky smile. 'Mum says I'm a strawberry blonde.'

'Then your mum's blind,' Donna mutters.

Sonia drops the pink tutu she was holding.

'Your hair's lovely, Sonia,' I tell her.

Sonia beams at me. 'Thanks, Abby! Which colour do *you* think I should get?'

It's weird; I've always known my place in the group – everyone likes me, I'm nice, and sometimes I can be quite funny. But my defining feature is *Tara's best friend*. If you invite me, you get super-cool Tara into the bargain. If you invite Tara – you have to have me along, like it or not. But today I feel like *I'm* the cool person. Gerry's arranged all of this. She knows her way around London, when none of us really had a clue, and she's turning this random shopping trip into a brilliant girls' day out. And because she keeps linking arms with me, asking my opinion, letting the others know she thinks I am the coolest girl in the world, I actually *feel* like the coolest girl in the world.

No more Boring Flabby Abby.

'So,' says Candy, 'are we all getting tutus?'

'Maybe we could wear them for the Winter Festival thing?' I suggest. Then I check the label. £30. 'Maybe not.'

'Total rip-off,' says Hannah, reading the label over my shoulder. 'I've seen them for £15 down the market.'

'But these ones are from Carnaby Street!' says Donna.

'Yeah,' says Sonia, grabbing up a light blue one. 'That makes them, like, designer.'

Donna and Sonia take their tutus and head up to the counter. Behind the counter is a woman with dyed black hair, shaved at the sides, and about seventeen piercings.

I jump up and push my tutu back on the shelf. I can't afford £30. I can't afford £15.

'What are you doing?' asks Gerry.

'Don't have any money,' I tell her. 'Spent it all getting the stuff for my elf mask.'

'But I don't want to get one if you're not.' She looks at me really seriously.

'You can get one,' I tell her. She doesn't have to wear everything I do.

Donna whips round. 'Are we getting these or aren't we?'

The woman behind the counter glares at us. She freezes, holding the tutu and the scanner in mid-air.

'You get yours,' says Gerry. 'We'll have to come back for ours another time.'

She looks at me and winks like I'm in on a secret – but I have no idea what she's on about. Something about the wink scares me. I've seen it before.

'So?' says Sonia, who will never do anything without the approval of Donna.

'Come on, girls,' says the woman behind the counter, who has clearly lost patience with us all messing her around and messing up her shop. 'I haven't got all day.'

'Well, I'm getting this one,' says Donna, and thrusts her tutu forward.

'What a relief,' the woman says under her breath.

Hannah and Indiana get one too.

Obi picks up a yellow one, but then puts it back. 'Nah,' she says. 'I don't think it's really me.'

I go and stand by Obi – solidarity in tutu-less-ness.

'Want to share a hot chocolate?' she asks me.

'Good plan,' I say. There's a cafe right next door. I call back to the others: 'Obi and I are going to get a hot chocolate.'

'Why bother?' says Hannah. 'You have about thirty Aeros in your bag.'

I blush. When Gerry showed up today she gave me a bumper box of Aeros; because 'I know they're your favourite.' I joked that one would have been fine. It was a nice gift, I suppose. She couldn't have known that I've gone off Aeros ever since that last day in Wales.

'But drinking chocolate is completely different to eating it,' I say.

Gerry nods. 'Totally!' she says. I can trust her to back me up.

'Meet us there, yeah?' I say to everyone.

Their faces look anxious.

'You're only next door though?' says Candy. 'You won't move from there, right?'

I love that they care where I'm going to be. The party is wherever *I* am. As Obi and I walk next door I feel really good about myself. Without Tara here, I can see how much I hide behind her when she is. I love her, she's my best friend, but now I can see how she sort of drowns me out. She's so sparkly that no one notices me beside her brightness. Now *I'm* the sparkly one.

Gerry is also super-sparkly. But unlike Tara, she carries me up there with her.

Obi and I find the biggest table they have – which is only for four people – and we get evil stares from the owner as we drag more chairs across.

The woman brings our one hot chocolate and eyes the six empty chairs. 'You and your friends can't all drink the same drink,' she says.

'They'll buy stuff,' I say. 'Promise.'

The woman rolls her eyes and walks away.

Obi takes a sip of the hot chocolate, then passes it to me.

'Gerry seems really nice,' she says.

'She is,' I say. 'Shame her boyfriend couldn't come in the end.'

Obi shrugs. 'Nah,' she says. 'Much better having just us girls, rather than Gerry's boyfriend and Lenny and all the other boys.'

Then Donna, Sonia, Indiana and Hannah come bursting in, giggling.

'Did you get them?' I call out.

'We did,' says Donna, holding her bulging bag in the air.

'But Gerry decided not to,' says Hannah.

Probably because I didn't. I should be flattered, but it's a bit of a responsibility having to look after her feelings as well as my own.

Candy and Gerry come into the cafe. Gerry is literally bouncing. 'Abbracadabra!' she yells.

People in the cafe start grumbling about 'noisy teenagers'.

'Gerry Christmas!' I say back, a little quieter, a greeting we worked out in Wales.

The girls laugh and crowd around the table. The woman comes over. 'Are you ordering anything?' she says. 'If not . . .'

'I'll have a mocha,' says Donna.

'Me too,' says Sonia.

Hannah, Indiana and Candy all order hot chocolates and then the woman looks at Gerry.

She still hasn't sat down and she's bouncing from foot to foot. 'Nothing for me, thanks,' she says.

'Then I'm going to have to ask you to leave,' the woman says.

'Oh, please let her stay!' I beg the woman. 'We'll be quiet.'

I hate people like her. But Gerry turns to me and winks again. That weird, scary wink. 'Not to worry, ma'am,' she says, smiling sweetly at the woman. 'Abby, come with me. I need to show you something.'

I feel bad for Gerry that the woman is chucking her out, so I stalk out of the cafe in a huff.

'Don't go anywhere!' Candy shouts.

'We'll just be outside,' I tell the others.

But as soon as we're out there, Gerry grabs my arm and runs around the corner with me. She pulls my arm so hard it hurts.

'Ow!' I say, but I'm laughing.

She leads me down a nasty alleyway with smelly bins and things on the floor that I don't want to look at.

'Normally I don't frequent such places,' I say in a posh voice.

'I know,' she says back, grinning. 'You're usually much more lowbrow.'

We both laugh.

'What's the big secret?' I ask her.

'I got you a present.' Gerry shrugs her backpack off and opens it. There's something bright and colourful in there, something lilac, and something else that's black.

'What's . . . ?' But I can see what it is now. It's made of netting. 'Did you get a tutu? Donna said you didn't.'

'Well, I did,' she says. She pulls out the black one. 'And I got you one too.'

'Oh my God!'

121

Gerry hands me the purple one. Her pupils are massive, and that scary look is back again. 'It'll go with the purple thing you're doing with your elf mask.'

I'd planned to have lilac shading over the eyes of my mask, like eyeshadow. I can't believe Gerry found a tutu to match it. 'That's so nice of you,' I say. They were so expensive. 'I could have got one in the market,' I tell her.

Gerry shakes her head. 'Don't be silly.' She starts putting her tutu on over her jeans. And throws mine to me so I start pulling it on over my leggings.

But there's a little hole in the skirt. 'Oh no, look . . .'

And then I realize. The way we ran. Gerry left with the others and they said she didn't get anything. Gerry's backpack is open and I can see a pair of scissors in there. She used them to cut out the security tag.

'Did you steal this?' I ask.

'No!' she says, looking horrified. Then she smiles. 'But let's not go past that shop on the way back, eh?' She winks at me again and it makes my stomach drop.

Stolen goods. I'm dealing in stolen goods.

And this isn't the first time.

Chapter 12

Me and Gerry were in the post office in Pembrokeshire. All they sold were a few sweets, stationery, toilet rolls, cereal, cheesy beach stuff, and one or two magazines. We'd already read the ones for teenagers, the glossy gossip ones too. That left the ones about fishing and boats, and about five on knitting.

'If you ever needed proof that this is the most boring place in the world, this magazine collection would be it!' Gerry said.

I whacked her on the arm. 'Shh!' I glanced at the lady behind the counter. 'She'll hear you.'

'Oh, what's she going to do? Call a meeting at the village hall?'

Even though she was being mean, I giggled. 'They might string us up as witches,' I whispered, enjoying being nasty.

I glanced over again. The woman seemed about

a hundred and seventy years old, with white hair, and her jumper looked like it had been knitted from one of the patterns in the magazine. Her eyes were closed behind her glasses.

'I hope she's not their last line of defence against bank robbers,' I whispered again.

Gerry turned to me and winked. 'Let's see, shall we?' She picked up an Aero. My favourite.

'No, thanks,' I said. I had had too much to eat already today and I didn't want to undo my hard work and become Flabby Abby again. 'I'm full.'

'So get it for later.' Gerry's whispering now and she passes the Aero to me.

I checked my purse. 'I only have £2 to get me through the rest of half-term.'

Gerry shrugged. There was something I didn't like in the way she looked. Something dark that I had seen a few times over the last week. She leaned forward and put her arm around me. 'Have you seen?' she said loudly. 'They have *Knitters' Weekly* – my absolute favourite!'

I giggled again. But then I felt Gerry's hand slip into my pocket and something drop inside.

The Aero.

Blood pulsed in my head. I turned and looked wide-eyed at Gerry. 'It's stealing,' I hissed.

'It's just a 60p chocolate bar.'

'It's still stealing though, isn't it?' I said to her.

She wrinkled her forehead. 'If they've been stupid enough to leave this old bag in charge of security, that's their fault.'

I felt a rush all over my body. I didn't like doing this – but it was something Boring Flabby Abby would never do. What would be the harm in taking one little chocolate bar from one little shop? Just to prove I could.

Head still spinning, I smiled weakly at Gerry.

'Dare you to go and talk to her,' she said.

'And say what?' My adrenalin was pumping.

'I don't know,' said Gerry. 'Ask her—'

'Can I help you girls with anything?'

I jumped. It was the old woman calling to us. Gerry pushed me towards her. I turned. I could feel the Aero in my pocket and wondered if I should simply pay for it. But for some reason, with Gerry watching, I didn't.

Instead I found myself imitating Gerry's dark look as I walked towards the woman behind the counter. 'We were just wondering if you had any more knitting magazines,' I asked.

The woman smiled. 'Keen knitters, are we?'

'Very!' I said. I heard Gerry snort behind me. 'We've read all the ones you have already – twice – and just wondered when you were getting more in.'

The woman looked so happy, truly believing we cared about knitting. I turned and smirked at Gerry, who smirked right back. Then she bent over and started gathering some stuff in her arms. She shooed me away to follow the woman, who had come out from behind the counter.

'If you've read all of those and would like more . . .' she was saying.

'Oh, we would, we would,' I said.

'How about giving crochet a try?' she said. She handed me a crochet magazine – people must actually buy this stuff! – and then reached for another. 'Or maybe . . . do you have a sewing machine at home? You could try making your own clothes.'

Actually, making my own clothes did sound cool. And the fact that the woman was being so helpful made me feel bad. 'Thanks,' I said to her, using my real voice. I wasn't going to be mean any more. She didn't deserve it. 'These look great. I don't have the money right now, but I'll come back when I do.'

I turned round to look for Gerry, but she wasn't in the shop.

'Thanks for the advice,' I said. I handed the magazines back to her and started towards the exit.

The woman smiled sweetly. 'You're welcome,' she said. 'And if you need any help with knitting, I'm your woman! Knitted this myself, you know.' She gestured at the jumper she was wearing. It was impressive, even if the design was a bit old-womany.

'It's lovely,' I said. Then, 'Bye.'

I turned and fled. Totally forgetting about the stolen chocolate bar in my pocket.

I threw it away as soon as I remembered it. And I haven't eaten an Aero since.

Chapter 13

We're all walking arm in arm from Carnaby Street down to Piccadilly Circus. There are eight of us, split four and four, taking up the whole space of the pavement. A man tuts as he has to step into the road to get round us.

'Sorry!' Gerry shouts at the top of her voice. 'We're on day release from the lunatic asylum.'

Sonia and Candy burst into fits of giggles.

The man turns around and winks, his bad mood gone. 'Then may I suggest a visit to the London Eye?'

Sonia giggles some more. Even Donna joins in.

We do look a little out there. Four of us are wearing brightly coloured tutus. Gerry managed to persuade me to put mine on. Even though I know it's stolen, I couldn't find a way to say no. Perhaps I can come back to the shop next week and leave it on the doorstep. I'm definitely not brave enough to give it back to the woman with the piercings.

I'm starting to wish Tara was here. She'd know what to do. But I haven't spoken to her. I haven't told her what I did in Wales – becoming a thief, and, worse still, letting Gerry think she's my best friend when Tara's always going to be my best friend forever. Yeah, Tara's been a bit rubbish recently, obsessing over Reece. But boyfriends come and go – mates are supposed to be forever. She's always been there for me. And Tara would never make me feel uncomfortable like Gerry does.

But it's not Gerry's fault either. She called us best friends and I never denied it.

Gerry's linked arms with Donna, Sonia and Candy just ahead of us. They stop. Which means me, Obi, Hannah and Indiana have to stop too.

'. . . like the Monkees,' she's saying.

'You want us to walk like monkeys?' asks Sonia.

'I'm not doing that,' says Donna.

Gerry laughs loudly, tipping her head right

back. 'Not like *monkeys*, like *the Monkees*,' she says. 'They're a sixties band. Here –' she straightens out their line. Then turns back to us and straightens us out too. 'Link arms.'

We do as we're told.

'And when you start walking put your left leg way out to the left, then the right way out to the right.' She makes a big sweeping movement with her left leg, stepping it so far left it crosses Donna's path. Then does the same with her right leg so it's in front of Sonia.

Donna, Sonia and Candy catch on and they start walking in this ridiculous foursome.

'Come on,' says Indiana, 'we'll do it too.'

We start walking like this, concentrating at first, then laughing. People are definitely staring at us, but it's quite funny now.

Our line is not as good as Gerry's. Partly because we haven't got Gerry leading us, and partly because I'm just not getting it. My legs keep going a different way to everyone else's.

'Hey!' says Indiana. 'Stop tripping me.'

I get the giggles. So do all the other girls.

Gerry starts singing at the top of her voice.

' 🎵 *Here we come . . . walking down the street . . .* 🎵 '

'I know this song,' says Candy.

I do too, and join in, singing along.

We pass a group of tourists who give us funny looks.

' 🎵 *Get the funniest looks from . . .* 🎵 '

We all crack up even harder. Even the people staring at us think Gerry's funny.

' 🎵 *Everyone we meet!* 🎵 '

We're yelling at the top of our voices.

Gerry bows at one of the bemused tourists. 'Welcome to London!' she cries.

'Gerry's so cool,' Indiana says to me.

I can't deny that. I wish there was a way I could sort this whole mess out so me and Gerry and Tara and all of the rest of the girls could all hang out.

'I can't believe she bought you that tutu,' Hannah whispers in my ear. 'I wish someone had bought *me* one.'

'She's really generous,' I say, choking back the guilt of accepting stolen property. I wish I could explain to Gerry that stealing's not OK, not ever.

Gerry turns around and it's clear she's been eavesdropping. 'I'm not normally this generous or this much fun – normally I am a right boring bum. It's Abby . . .'

The girls all look at me with new-found respect.

'Right backatcha, Gerry,' I say.

The girls smile.

'This is what best friends do,' Gerry says.

Now the others look at each other. Candy's mouth drops open. I try to hold my smile but I can tell it's wobbling.

Donna narrows her eyes at me. I psychically plead with her: *Please don't*. I know it will embarrass me. And it will really hurt Gerry.

I start us all walking again. We round the busy corner of Brewer Street and hit Piccadilly Circus – packed on a Saturday afternoon.

'Gerry . . . ?' says Donna, and she draws the word out so long that I know what she's about to do. 'Have you met Tara? She goes to our school.

She was going to come today, but she had a family thing . . .'

'Tara,' says Gerry, frowning. 'Was she the girl at the hospital?' she asks me. She's wearing her dark expression.

'Yeah,' I say. 'And the thing is . . .' This is it. I should just tell Gerry now and get it over with. If she doesn't forgive me, then, well, I deserve it.

Gerry turns away. Something's caught her eye. 'Hey! I've got a brilliant idea.' Smiling brightly. Dark expression gone. 'Can someone lend me three pounds? I'll give it back in, like, five minutes.'

'What do you need it for?' asks Candy.

'You'll see,' she says. Candy and Obi each give her some change. 'Meet me at Eros.' She points to the fountain packed with loads of people, mostly tourists, taking photos of the busy street and flashing adverts above.

Gerry runs off into a stationery shop.

'So,' Donna says to me, 'you and Gerry are BFFs now?'

Sonia puts one hand on her hip. 'Does Tara know?'

We cross the road so we're standing in front of Eros. 'Wow, Donna,' I say, trying to shrug it off. 'You can have more than one friend, you know. I mean, I'm friends with all of you guys, and Tara is pretty fine about that.'

'But Gerry said you were her *best* friend,' says Obi. 'You can only have one best friend.'

'Of course, and I do,' I say, my voice shaking a little. 'And it's Tara. No contest.'

I'm just lucky that none of them have seen the bracelet Gerry's wearing, covered by the sleeve of her coat.

'That's not what Gerry seems to think,' says Donna, loving that she gets to rub it in.

'Just because I'm Gerry's best friend, doesn't mean that she's mine,' I tell her.

Obi frowns. I suppose that was a pretty heartless thing to say.

'I'd be Gerry's best friend,' Hannah mutters.

'Don't say anything to Gerry. Please. Why would you want to hurt her feelings like that?' I beg them. 'Promise me you won't go on about it.'

Indiana, Hannah, Sonia, Obi and Candy nod, but Donna's staying suspiciously quiet.

Gerry joins us, with something big and flat tucked under her arm.

'What've you got there?' I call out, making an effort to sound excited.

She smiles the same smile as she did that night on the cliff-top. I recognize it. The darkness and big pupils are back and it makes me shudder. With Gerry you have to expect the unexpected . . . and it's not always good.

'It's a money-spinner,' she says.

She sits herself down on the stone steps in front of Eros. It must be cold on her bum – it's November – but she doesn't seem to notice. She pulls a marker pen out of her bag and scrawls:

**Portraits
£4
5 minutes**

I didn't know Gerry could draw. Which is weird, because she knows how into art I am. She saw my sketch pad.

'Now go and drum me up some business,' she says, wafting us away into the masses.

The girls look at me for an explanation.

'Is she really good at art or something?' Obi asks me.

I shrug. 'I don't know. I guess she must be.'

Candy and Indiana get into it. They approach a couple of tourists, point at Gerry and mime drawing. The tourists shake their head, but at least they're smiling. I pass a few people, force myself to tap them on the shoulder and point over to Gerry. She's chewing on the end of her pen.

Donna grabs Sonia and points to three cute-looking guys, definitely way older than us. 'I'm doing this for the team,' she says as she struts off. 'You can't tell Lenny.' She stands in front of the boys. 'Now, you look like a group who should be immortalized.' She bats her eyelashes.

The boys look her up and down. 'What?' one of them says.

'My friend over there wants to do your portraits,' she says. 'Only £4.'

'Much cheaper than the other people offering caricatures,' says Sonia. And it's true. There are other artists around and they're charging, like, £10. They are also starting to give us dirty looks. Maybe they don't like that we're stealing their business.

But when I look back to Gerry, Indiana has managed to drag someone over. The couple look Chinese and from the hand gestures Indiana's doing, I'm guessing they don't speak English.

We all crowd round. 'This is so awesome, Gerry,' I say to her. 'Why didn't you say you could do this kind of thing?'

'Shh!' says Gerry, smiling at me but making a face that tells me to be cool. 'This is supposed to look like a professional gig.' The wild look is still there. It fills me with dread.

The Chinese man and his wife don't pick up on it.

'We're going to need the money up front.' Gerry puts her hand out, then holds up four fingers. 'We've had trouble with runners in the past,' Gerry said this really loudly as if that's going to help with the translation.

The Chinese couple start nodding and the woman fishes around in her bumbag for the coins.

Gerry pockets the money, smiles, and then frowns at them, concentrating. She holds her pen up in the air to measure them. This is something I've seen people do on TV but never seen done in real life. 'Now, girls,' Gerry says to us, as she sticks her tongue out and draws a line down the page. 'Prepare yourselves . . . the magic is just about to happen . . .'

There's a feeling in my stomach like I'm going up on a roller coaster. I can't tell if I'm excited or terrified.

Gerry draws a line over the top of the line she's already drawn. I can't see what it's going to become yet but she keeps looking from the couple, whose fixed smiles are quite manic, back to her page again.

'Are you ready?' she whispers under her breath.

'We're ready,' I say.

'Ready!' shouts a woman standing next to me. Gerry's brought in a bit of a crowd. Three or four tourists have joined our circle, looking at what Gerry's about to do.

'Go!' shouts Gerry.

She drops the pad of paper, scrambles to her feet, and runs.

I stand there for a second. I'm waiting to see what my mad friend is going to do next.

But she's gone. Just gone. She doesn't even look back.

'Go!' shouts Donna. She looks petrified. She sets off running after Gerry. Sonia instantly follows her.

I feel sick. Terrified. Definitely not excited.

Hannah looks at me, looks at the Chinese couple who are searching all around them, presumably for Gerry. Maybe they're looking for the police.

'Hey . . .' the Chinese man says. But Gerry's gone and none of us have reacted quickly enough to catch her.

'I'm not getting in trouble for this,' says Hannah, and she runs in a different direction.

The Chinese woman's face crumples as she realizes what's just happened. The three tourists standing round look at me.

'Did you know that girl?' one of them asks. 'Did she just take their money?'

I shake my head.

'What shall we do?' Obi whispers to me.

'I'm not leaving,' I say.

'Me neither,' says Indiana. 'Bad karma.'

A bit of a commotion has started up around us. The Chinese couple are still looking around. They seem more confused than angry and it breaks my heart. I can't believe Gerry's done this.

Actually, I think I can. I haven't known her for long, but this isn't totally out of character.

'How much money do you have?' I ask Obi and Indiana.

I start scrabbling around in my purse. I have just under a pound. Indiana drops two pound coins and some small change into my hand, Obi adds some silver.

I hand it all to the Chinese woman. 'Sorry,' I say, even though I know she can't understand. 'I'm really sorry. Here's your money back.'

Indiana and Obi say sorry too, and then we turn and head out of Piccadilly as fast as we can, all of us quiet as we process what just happened.

I look down at my tutu. I don't want it. I try

to think of a place where I can take it off and dump it.

'Hey!' says one of the fit boys Donna was flirting with. 'Did that girl just steal from that old couple?'

'Is she a friend of yours?' asks another one.

Me, Obi and Indiana do not slow down as we head to the underground. 'No,' I say without turning back to them. 'She is definitely not a friend of mine.'

And that's it. Gerry and I are over.

Chapter 14

'Why didn't you invite us along with you?' asks Joel.

We're in room 11 for geography, but Mr Raza hasn't arrived yet so we're all sitting around chatting.

'Yeah,' says Lenny. 'Sounds like it was fun.' He's sitting on a desk.

Donna's on a chair in front of him. She tilts her head so it's resting on his thigh. 'Aww, sorry, hun – it was kind of a girls' thing.'

Lenny smiles down at her. I'm not sure what the deal is with those two – I know they aren't officially a couple or else Donna would have said. But there's definitely something unofficial going on.

Joel pouts. 'Next time you have to invite me, yeah?' He says this to me and I have to will my face not to blush.

'Actually it was a bit of a nightmare,' says Obi, shaking her head at the memory.

Tara joins in, telling Reece, 'Apparently that girl Abby met on holiday – Gerry – stole some money off some old couple.'

I'm ashamed just to think about it. There is a lot to be said for Boring Flabby Abby who hides behind Sparkly Tara. Much better than New Abby, who steals and hangs round with a thieving nutcase.

'Really?' says Reece, looking at me. 'Why would she do that?'

'I'm not her guardian,' I snap. But I've been wondering the same thing. What's wrong with Gerry that she thinks it's OK to steal? And why is she so needy?

Indiana looks at Hannah and the rest of them. 'I can't believe you ran off after her. Me, Obi and Abby had to pay those poor people back,' she says.

Tara crosses her arms and looks at Indiana. 'Well, I can't believe this Gerry girl did that and you all *still* friended her on Facebook.'

Indiana seems a bit embarrassed.

I can't believe it either. I thought after what Gerry did, she would be out of my life for good.

Now they all look a little awkward. Donna raises her head from Lenny's thigh and says, 'I didn't mean to,' she says. 'I just saw a girl asking to be my friend and accepted it.'

'Because you are so desperate for friends,' Obi mutters.

'No,' she says. But Donna's got over a thousand friends on Facebook and I doubt she'd recognize half of them if they came and knocked on her door.

'Why did *you* friend her?' she throws back to Obi.

Obi's reaction is much more believable. 'Do you know why?' she says. 'Because I thought she might apologize!' Obi is still fuming and I don't blame her. 'She owes me money.'

'And me,' says Indiana.

'And me,' says Candy. 'I paid for that pad of paper.'

Gerry did apologize. Eventually. She rang me five minutes after it happened, but I was underground so she left a message. She was laughing, asking where we should meet up. No apology. It took me ignoring five texts and three calls for her to finally get it.

Then her messages changed.

'I'm sorry . . . I thought you were all going to run too . . . I should have let you all in on the plan . . .'

I meant to ignore her, but that one got me too annoyed. I texted her back:

It's not that you left me behind. It's that you even did it in the first place! You conned that poor old couple!!!

Then she tried to say she was pranking us. She claimed she went back to Eros and looked for the couple to return the money and let them in on the joke, but they were gone.

I want to believe her. But I'm not sure if I should. Especially as I'm 99.9% sure she stole those tutus from that shop too, just like she pushed me into stealing the Aero bar.

I'm going to go back to how life was two

weeks ago – forget about New Abby and forget Gerry ever happened.

Mr Raza comes into the room. 'Sorry I'm a bit late,' he says. 'As compensation I'll pretend I didn't see all those mobile phones out,' he says with a warning in his voice. 'Sit down, please.'

Everyone gets up and moves to their seats.

'Abby!' Joel shout-whispers at me. 'Sit here.' He pats the chair next to him.

Oh my God! Joel wants me to sit next to him! I glance at Tara – she knows how exciting this is for me. She wiggles her eyebrows and smiles.

'Sorry, Joel,' I say, trying to hide how happy I am. 'You know I always sit with my best friend.' I grab Tara and put my arm in hers.

She reaches up and subtly squeezes my hand. 'You could have sat next to him if you wanted,' she whispers. 'I wouldn't have minded.'

'Nah,' I say. 'You're my best friend and I want to sit next to you.' Joel will wait.

'Sit next to your best friend?' Donna repeats, doing a fake version of me. 'But Gerry doesn't even go to this school.'

She's such a stirrer.

'What do you mean?' says Tara.

'Ignore her,' I say, feeling my face get hot.

'Settle down, class,' Mr Raza says.

Donna gets out her books and pens from her bag. She's not even looking at Tara when she says, 'Gerry told us all how she and Abby are best friends now.'

I hate Donna sometimes.

'Is that true?' Tara asks me.

'No!' I say. Well, she *did* say that. But I didn't say I was *her* best friend. Not that time at least. But it doesn't matter any more. I'm never speaking to Gerry again. So if Donna will just let it drop, everything will be fine.

'Sit down now,' Mr Raza says, glaring at us.

Tara and I sit. Tara starts to pout; she looks really hurt. 'You're not going off with her, are you?' she whispers.

'No!' I say. 'I don't even want to be friends with her any more.' It's nice to be telling Tara the absolute truth. I should have done it from the very beginning. Unfortunately, the look on Tara's face says she doesn't believe me.

I put my pencil case on the desk and root for my phone in my bag.

'Today,' says Mr Raza, 'we will be continuing to look at cloud formations . . .'

'I'll defriend her.'

I'm expecting Tara to tell me that I don't need to go as far as that, but she doesn't. She looks at me expectantly. I've never defriended anyone, but the truth is I'll be happy to defriend Gerry. Even if she texts and calls, I'll just ignore her until she gives up.

With my phone hidden under the desk I go straight to Gerry's Facebook profile, expecting to find a defriend button there, but I can't see one. But I've got a notification and I can't help myself. I have to check it.

Abby Gardner fancies Joel Owens.

I gasp.

'What?' whispers Tara.

Posted by Gerry Barnes.

I show Tara the post and she puts her hand over her mouth. 'When did she write that?'

Twenty minutes ago.

As soon as she sees what I'm doing, Donna grabs her phone too.

Now *she* gasps.

'What did I say about phones?!' says Mr Raza, shouting now.

'Like!' Donna says out loud. Then she throws her phone in her bag. 'Sorry, Mr Raza.'

Oh God!

First Gerry steals my friendship bracelet, forcing me to lie to my best friend. Then she makes me a criminal. Now she's ruining everything at school too! She's just told the world I fancy Joel. I want to die with embarrassment.

I wish I had never met Gerry. How do I get her out of my life?

Chapter 15

Next lesson is chemistry. By the time we get there, *everyone* knows.

I bury my head and try to concentrate on the liquid in the beaker, but it's hard when all I can hear is whispering and I'm pretty sure it's not about the boiling point of copper sulphate solution.

When Mr Davidson's back is turned I slyly check my phone again. Four more likes. Two people have shared it. I can't believe Gerry's done this to me!

Tara's looking over my shoulder. 'I can't believe Gerry did this to you.'

I love that Tara thinks exactly the same way.

'And I can't believe Donna went and shared it on her wall,' I whisper back.

'Can't you?'

Tara's right, Donna can be a cow sometimes.

But she's not the real problem here. I need to cut Gerry off and cut her off completely. Before she does any more damage to my already rubbish life.

Mr Davidson turns back and I have to hide my phone under my books.

Too late. He raises an eyebrow at me. 'I hope that wasn't a phone I saw,' he says. 'All equipment in the lab gets cleaned in the pressure cooker.'

This is a threat that he's used loads of times, and I think it's a joke so I smile. 'Sorry.' As soon as he looks away I turn to Tara. 'I'm going to ask her to remove the post.'

'Ask her why she did it in the first place,' says Tara. 'Then ask her to keep the hell out of your business.'

I nod. When Mr Davidson walks over to the other side of the lab to check up on whatever silliness Lenny is getting up to with Danny Russell, I slide my phone back out again. I text Gerry:

Why did you post that on your wall?! Everyone at school has seen it. Take it down!

Gerry replies instantly:

Everyone's seen it? You're welcome!!! x x

I show Tara and she clenches her teeth. 'What's her problem?'

I start writing a text back, along the lines of what Tara just said, but Mr Davidson comes over and catches me.

'Give that to me,' he says, his hand out.

'Sorry, Mr Davidson,' I say, and drop my phone into my bag before he can put it in the pressure cooker.

'Will you two please just concentrate on your chemistry and not your social lives.'

Phil Horner pipes up. 'But Abby's social life is filled with chemistry, Mr Davidson . . .' I feel myself go bright red, '. . . with Joel Owens.'

Everyone bursts out laughing and starts making '*Oooh*' and kissy noises. Someone even wolf-whistles. I can't bear to look at Joel. Poor guy, he's suffering as much as I am, and he's just the victim in all this. He doesn't fancy anyone. He didn't befriend a deranged girl who posts people's secrets online for the world to see.

'Be quiet, class!' Mr Davidson says.

I stick my hand up. 'Can I go to the toilet, please, Mr Davidson?'

Mr Davidson frowns, but he's a nice teacher really – he can see I'm being humiliated by thirty people all at once. He sighs. And that's all I need. I grab my bag and run out of the room.

Behind me I can hear sniggering. And also Tara asking, 'Can I go with her?'

But Mr Davidson's all out of sympathy. 'I'm sure Abby can navigate the complexities of going to the toilet on her own.' Which gets more laughs from the class.

Probably best if I *do* do this on my own. I'm going to call Gerry and tell her that she's not my best friend, she's not even my friend. I want her to take everyone I know off her Facebook – they're *my* friends, not hers – and as soon as she has, I'll defriend her. I'm going to block her on Instagram too. And then I'm going to tell her to delete my number from her phone.

I slam into the girls' toilets. I don't use our meeting room – instead I lock myself in one of the loo cubicles and call her.

'Hi, Abby!' Gerry shrieks as she picks up.

'Gerry, I want to talk to—'

'I'm with Mack,' she says. It must be break time at her school. 'Want to say hello to Mack?'

I do not want to say hello to Mack! But it's too late, 'Hi, Abby.' Mack's voice comes booming down the phone. 'What's up?'

I feel a bit awkward now. I'm angry, but not with Mack. It's not his fault his girlfriend is crazy. 'Not much . . .'

There is a bit of struggling and laughter on the other end of the phone, then Gerry's back on. 'Can't have you two flirting in front of my face!' she says cheerfully.

This hasn't put me off one bit. 'I need to talk to you, Gerry,' I say.

She goes quiet. She can tell by my voice that I'm not a happy bunny. 'Okaaaaay,' she says.

'Why did you post that stuff on my wall?

Now everyone knows I fancy Joel. And Joel knows. Even my chemistry teacher knows.'

'Huh?'

'Someone made a joke in class,' I say.

Gerry laughs. 'Well, I'm sorry about *that*.'

'So why did you do it?!' I can feel myself getting hotter. I'm furious, and the fact that she's being so calm is making me mad.

'I'm not sorry about posting it,' she says.

'You've ruined my chances with Joel!' I yell. 'He can't even look at me now.' I can't look at him to see if he's looking at me, but I'm sure he won't be.

'Have I ruined your chances . . .' she says, sounding all cryptic, '. . . or have I just improved them?'

'You've *ruined* them!'

'You were never going to make the move,' she says, her voice so light it floats. 'This way, at least he knows.'

'I didn't want him to know!'

'Are you kidding?' she says, like *I'm* the crazy person. 'Joel would be mad not to fancy you! You're the best.'

It's hard to be furious with someone who's so complimentary.

'Boys are just as nervous as girls when it comes to making the move,' she says. 'Am I right, Mack?'

There's a grunting noise.

'Now Joel knows you like him. If he likes you, he'll ask you out.'

Trouble is, there's no way that someone as great as Joel would like me. I mean, he likes me . . . but not like that. I am *friend* material, not *girl*friend material.

'But he doesn't, that's the problem,' I say, quieter now.

'Then he's an idiot,' she says. 'And you don't want to go out with an idiot.'

My lip starts to go wobbly and I feel myself starting to cry. 'Yeah, I do . . .' I say in a whisper.

'Come on, Abs. Forget about him. He's an idiot who doesn't deserve you. We could introduce you to one of Mack's friends, couldn't we, Mack?'

The idea of being set up with a hot friend

of Mack's feels exciting for about a nanosecond. Gerry's nice . . . or at least, she's nice to me. But she's unpredictable. And a thief. The thought of spending any more time with Gerry is actually pretty scary.

'Do you know what, Gerry?' I say, and I take a deep breath. 'I think I'd prefer it if you stayed out of my business.'

Deathly silence from the other end of the phone.

'Completely,' I finish. I can hear blood pulsing in my ears. I have never been so harsh to anyone.

'I'm sorry, Abby,' she says. Her voice is trembling. 'I was only—'

'What you did this weekend, stealing that money from those people—'

'It was a joke!' she yelps. 'I gave the money back.'

'I thought you said you couldn't find them,' I remind her.

'No, I found them. It just took ages,' she says. 'I gave them the money and they were really angry. You lot spoilt the joke by freaking out. It made it look like we were stealing money when we weren't—'

'*We* weren't stealing money. You were. We had no idea!' I huff at her. I'm not used to feeling angry like this, but actually it makes what I'm about to say easier. 'Gerry, I would prefer it if you just left me alone from now on.'

'Is Tara making you do this?' she says, her voice deep and gravelly.

'No.' What a weird thing to ask.

'Did she find out we're best friends now?'

'No,' I say again. 'And, Gerry, we're not best friends, OK? I've only known you for like—'

'But the bracelet. What if I showed it to Tara? Then she'd get the message.'

Is she threatening me?

'And I have something else that you wouldn't want me to show Tara, don't I?'

I can't think what she's talking about, but I'm filled with dread. 'Look, Gerry, I'm sorry if there was some misunderstanding, but I don't want to be friends with you any—'

'Huh? Sorry? What?' she says. 'I can't

hear you. The bell just went for the next class.'

I didn't hear any bell.

'Mack and I have been bunking, but Mrs Lamb is well on top of things.'

'Gerry . . .' I say. I'm not stupid. I know she's trying to get out of this.

'Can we talk later?' she says. 'Gotta go. Love ya. Mack says bye too.' And the phone goes dead.

I am so frustrated that I could kick the door. That didn't go quite as I planned, but at least I've started the conversation. It'll make it easier to end it tonight.

I just hope she was joking about showing Tara the bracelet. And whatever else it is she says I've done.

I hide out in the toilets for another ten minutes – splashing water on my face and brushing my hair. I wait until there are about three minutes of class left before heading back.

When I finally push the door to the chemistry lab, the class is silent, all writing up the notes from the lesson.

Mr Davidson says, 'Are you all right, Abigail?'

I nod. I can see some of the boys smirking.

'Then sit down,' he says. 'Tara has the sheet you need to fill in for homework.'

Tara's beaming when I sit. 'You OK?' she whispers.

'Yeah,' I whisper back. 'Are *you*?' She looks as if she's drunk five cans of Red Bull or something – all smiley and squirmy. She nods to a folded-up piece of paper on my desk.

'*From Joel,*' she mouths.

I can't believe it! '*Joel?*' I say, just to make sure.

She nods again.

'*What does it say?*'

She shrugs.

Maybe he's telling me to stay away. That he can't stand the fact that everyone's talking about him and Boring Flabby Abby.

I dare to sneak a look over at where Joel is sitting, but he's writing, head down.

Knowing Joel, he wouldn't be mean about it. The note will say something about him being flattered or something, but he's not looking for a girlfriend. Some lie like that.

Then he looks up at me and smiles, then blushes and looks back down.

I pull the paper beneath the desk and open it. There is his scrawling, boysy handwriting.

Want to hang out tomorrow night?

I clench my mouth shut to stop myself from squealing out loud. That's all it says — no romantic declarations of love, or poems, or deep and meaningfuls . . . but he knows I like him, and he wants to hang out. And that's the best news in the entire world.

Tara's studying my face. I slide the note over so she can read it. She lets out a little squeak. Faces turn to look at us so we quickly look back down at our books and pretend to write.

She squeezes my arm. We both know what this means — double dates, endless gossiping, total inside information. I will be going out with my best friend's boyfriend's best friend.

Tara was wrong, and Gerry was completely and totally one-hundred-per-cent right. She's so much more worldly-wise than we are. I should have trusted her. She knew exactly what she was doing, posting that on my wall.

If Gerry was here, I would give her the biggest fattest hug right now.

Chapter 16

Tara stands in front of me and applies a last flick of mascara on to my lashes. She takes a step back to inspect her work. 'You look amazing, Abby,' she says.

I push her aside to look in the mirror. I have to admit, I do look pretty OK.

Joel and I have arranged to meet at Starbucks in the centre at six, then go to see a film. Tara and I had just enough time to leg it back to my house to change into a different outfit and do my hair and make-up.

No one is home, as usual. It means that Mum can't make a big deal about the fact I have an absolutely real and total actual date. But I guess it is a big deal. Joel found out I liked him and *then* asked me out.

'I can't believe you're going on a date,' says Tara.

'It's amazing, isn't it?'

'Reece and I have never even been on a proper date.' Tara sticks out her lip in a gigantic pout.

'What about that time . . . ?' But now I come to think of it, I can't remember any time that Reece and Tara have arranged to meet then got dressed up to go to a movie or dinner or anything. They've done those things, but I've always been there, and Joel and Lenny and most of the other girls. None of us have been on a one-on-one date yet, and I can't believe it's me who's going first.

This would never have happened if I hadn't met Gerry. I've completely forgiven her for her weirdness, and I told her so when I called her back. She's definitely a little strange, but she's got my best interests at heart. She'd never do anything to hurt me. And as she's such a good friend I've decided to give her the benefit of the doubt.

'You're so lucky, Abs,' she says. 'Tell me what it's like. I need every tiny detail.'

I give her a hug. 'Tell Reece you want him

to ask you on date. Or you could even ask him.'

For the first time since we were about four years old, *I* feel like the wise old woman out of the two of us.

'Mind if I give Gerry a call?' I ask Tara.

Tara sits on the bed with a *whump*. 'Sure,' she says. 'Tell her I said hi. . . even though I've never met her.'

'You will,' I say.

I call Gerry, and for the first time ever there's no answer. I text her.

About to go on my date. Wish me luck!!! x x

Usually there is a text back in seconds. But this time, nothing.

'Maybe she's busy,' I say to Tara.

Tara just nods, a weak smile on her face.

I take a deep breath. 'Project *Romance Joel* is go-go-go.'

Tara jumps up and posts her arm through mine. 'Come on then,' she says, walking me downstairs.

'What do I do if he asks me to be his girlfriend?' My heart's beating really fast.

'Er . . . how about . . . you say *yes*.'

'Of course I'll say yes. But how should I say it? Should I just nod politely and say, "yes," like, *that will be acceptable*, or should I jump up and down and scream and grab him round the neck like a TV-talent-show winner?'

Tara laughs. 'Try somewhere in between the two.'

'OK,' I say, too nervous to laugh along.

'And what if he tries to kiss me?'

'Do you want to kiss him?'

'Yes! I think. It's just . . . you know, I've never kissed anyone before.'

We're at the bottom of the stairs now and Tara turns to me. Things are back to the way they were, Tara counselling me through things she has more experience in.

'Don't worry too much about it,' she says.

'But how do you actually do it?'

'You've seen it on TV, right? And you know that there are tongues involved, right? Well, start by doing it like they do on TV . . . Then when you have been going out for ages, like me and Reece have . . .'

Once again, she's back on Reece. And she doesn't even realize how silly she sounds – they've only been going out for two weeks! That's hardly ages.

'. . . you will work out your own way,' she continues, 'For example, me and Reece start off quite slow—'

I shove my hands over my ears. 'La la la la! Too much information!' I yell.

Tara giggles. 'You asked!'

I open the front door, quickly do my check for keys, purse and phone. It's all there. I turn off the hall light and close the door behind me.

Tara looks back at the empty house. 'How's Becky doing?'

I harden myself. 'She's doing OK,' I say. 'As well as can be expected. In fact . . . could you come with me to the hospital after school tomorrow?'

'Of course,' she says. 'You know I love visiting Bex.'

'It's more that . . . I need to ask the doctor something. And it's something serious. I need you there.'

'What is it?'

I can feel the Becky Lump rising in my throat. The thought of giving up my kidney for my sister fills me with terror, but I know I have to. My eyes are prickling, and since Tara went to so much effort to do my make-up, I am not going to cry and ruin it all now. 'Can we talk about it later?'

She nods.

We're at the end of the road. Starbucks is in one direction, Tara's house the other.

'Want me to walk you there?' she asks.

Much as I love Tara, I can't have her walking me to my first date like she walked me to our first day at Hillcrest. I can't be in Tara's shadow, tonight of all nights.

Luckily she gets it as soon as I think it. 'I could hold your hand? Give you away at the altar? Ask Joel his intentions?'

I laugh. 'Thanks, but no thanks.'

She gives me a big hug. 'You look absolutely

gorgeous and you're going to knock his socks off.'

'Thanks, Tara.' I take a deep breath.

'I'll text you as soon as I'm home,' I say at the exact same time as she says, 'Text me as soon as you're home.'

I give her a thumbs-up and make my way down to the town centre.

My first date. All my life I'll always remember my first date, and this is it. I'll always remember Joel. His scruffy clothes, his messy hair. The way that whatever time of day it is, he looks like he's just woken up. I'm excited and nervous – like being on the roller coaster again. I know Tara says she wishes she'd been on a proper date with Reece, but I kind of wish everyone else was here. My heart's hammering like mad. What are we going to talk about? What will I say to him? What if it's just hours and hours of complete silence? At least in the cinema it won't be too obvious. But there's before and after. I'm not sure I'm cut out for talking to boys.

My phone rings. Maybe Tara's going to talk me to Starbucks.

It's Gerry.

'Hellooooo,' I call to her like a 1950s phone operator. 'You are speaking to a very nervous girl heading off for her very first date. How can I help you?'

There's a sniff on the other end of the line. Then nothing.

'Hello?'

More sniffing and more nothing.

'Gerry?'

'Abby!' she says, and then she gulps. 'I just phoned . . . to . . . Oh yeah – good luck on your date with Joel.'

'Thanks,' I say. 'I don't know whether I want to go or want to run a mile. I keep turning back—'

'I forgot it was tonight.'

She forgot it was tonight?!!! She's the one who made it all happen, and that was only yesterday! 'How could you forget? I've been texting you all day!' I say. 'And you have my social calendar synced with yours.'

I start to laugh. On the other end of the phone, Gerry makes this noise that's sort of terrifying. Like she's trying to breathe through water.

'Are you OK?' I ask.

The line goes quiet. 'I'm fine,' she says, but the cheeriness in her voice sounds completely forced. 'What film are you going to see? Is it one where you can dive into his arms if it gets scary?'

In the background I hear people walking around. And some sort of announcement. From the sounds of it, I'm guessing she's in a train station.

'Where are you?'

She hesitates. 'I'm at home.'

'No, you're not. Where are you?'

The announcement in the background mentions something about a train to Shepperton.

'Are you in Wimbledon?' She's come all the way to see me.

'No . . . yes . . .' Gerry bursts into tears. 'Abby!' she wails. 'Mack's dumped me!'

'Oh my God!' Poor Gerry. She's totally and completely in love with Mack. And from everything she's said, I thought he was in love with her too. 'What happened?'

There's lots of gulping noises. 'He cheated . . . on Saturday . . . You know, when we all met up . . .'

On Saturday when we went to London. Mack was supposed to come, but couldn't at the last minute. 'I thought he was at football practice?'

'I'm so stupid,' she says. 'Why would there be a *football emergency*?'

'So what was he really doing?'

'He was out with this girl – Ellie Poole – and apparently they snogged and everything.'

That is so awful.

'Worst thing is, Ellie was supposed to be my friend!' Her voice gets deeper, angrier. The gravel is back. 'Just goes to show you should be careful who you trust.'

I check my watch. 'Are you here now?' I ask her. It won't take me a second to stop off at the station, give her a massive hug, make sure she's OK, before I go on to meet Joel.

'Don't be ridiculous,' she says. 'You have your date.'

'Don't *you* be ridiculous,' I tell her. 'You've travelled hours to come and see me.'

'No way!' she says. 'I'm getting on the next train home. I shouldn't have come. I should have remembered. I'm sorry, Abby.'

I get to the end of the high street. 'You need me. I'll be there in thirty seconds.'

Gerry sighs, and it sounds like relief. 'One hug,' she says. 'Then I'm going.'

'See you in twenty-nine . . . twenty-eight . . . twenty seven . . .' I can hear her sniffly laugh as I hang up.

I check my phone. It's five to six. I can talk to Gerry for a while, turn up five minutes late to meet Joel – treat 'em mean and keep 'em keen *blah blah blah* – and then we can have our romantic date.

Gerry's standing in the station. She's looking down at her phone, her red curls covering her face. When she looks up she sees me straight away. 'Abby!' she says. Her face is all wet.

I run over and give her a hug. 'You poor thing. Are you OK?'

She shakes her head, even though it's buried into my neck. 'No,' she wails. 'He's such a git.'

'That's right,' I say. 'That's the way to think. He's a git and he doesn't deserve you.'

'I know what you're saying is right,' she says. 'But he was a fit git,' she adds, as if he's dead. 'He was, like, the best-looking boy in my school. And the best kisser.'

'But if he's done that to you, he's an idiot,' I say, remembering her advice to me. 'You don't want to go out with an idiot.'

Gerry nods.

'And this girl – Ellie Poole – she was a friend of yours?' I ask.

Gerry pulls away from me and gives a stare so filled with hate it actually scares me. 'She *was*,' she says. Her pupils are massive. 'We've been friends for years. But she's always been jealous of me. I guess it's because my parents are still together and she's never even met her dad. I have a bigger house and everything. I've always been a bit more popular with the boys. People say I'm prettier . . . but I don't know. If that was true, why would Mack run off with her?'

I've heard about girls who do this to other girls. 'I'm so sorry, Gerry.'

She's sobbing on my shoulder and I let her. But then I see the time. It's five past.

She cranes her neck back; she's caught me checking my watch. 'You need to go,' she says, swiping away the tears that are streaming down her face. 'You don't need my dramas on your plate tonight.'

'No . . .' I say, feeling bad that she saw me checking. 'I should just text Joel to say I'm going to be a bit late though.'

Gerry pushes me away. 'You go,' she says, her voice shaking. 'I'll be fine . . . on my owww . . .'

But she can't even get the final word out because she's crying so hard.

I step back towards her. I can't leave her. Not like this.

'Come with me.'

Gerry frowns. 'Ha! Who ordered the gooseberry?' she says in a heavy American accent like a woman who works at a diner.

Gerry is amazing to be able to make jokes at a time like this. 'Just come,' I say. 'Have a coffee. Meet Joel.'

'I'm sure he'll be thrilled,' she says flatly.

'He will!' I assure her. 'Besides, you'll be doing me a favour.'

'By ruining your chance for a snog?'

'No!' I say, and nudge her gently with my shoulder. 'I'm really nervous. With you there it will totally calm the situation down and make it less scary. You know how brilliant you are at talking to boys.'

Gerry pulls her mouth to one side. She's considering it. And I'm not sure how I feel. What I said just now was true – I am scared, I do want her there to break the ice. But also I feel like the nervousness is part of the package. This is my first date, and it won't be a real date if she tags along.

'Are you sure?' she says. And she looks so sad. She unzips her coat and I see she's wearing a lacy green top. Just like my one. But I don't want to be like Donna and get annoyed about something as stupid as that.

I'll still have my date. Gerry will get a coffee with us, then Joel and I will head off to the cinema to hold hands and stuff. We'll talk about the film and about how great Gerry is. He might be able to offer Gerry some boy advice about Mack.

'Of course,' I say.

'Thanks, Abby,' she says. 'You're the best friend a girl could have.'

I gulp. I tried to tell her about the best-friend thing but she seems to have blocked it out. I need to remind her that Tara is my best friend. Now, however, as she's dabbing her face with powder to cover up the tears, is not the time.

And as I head off on my very first date, with a boy I've liked for months and a girl I met two weeks ago, I'm thinking I've lost control of this.

Chapter 17

'You had a date?' Becky asks me. 'With a boy?'

'Keep your nose out, you.' I shoot her a warning glare.

'A date?' says Mum, looking up from her book. 'Who had a date?'

'Thanks for that, Tara,' I say, giving her a fake annoyed look.

Tara's smiling sweetly, laughing at my embarrassment. 'Abby did.' She wiggles her eyebrows.

We're all sitting round Becky's hospital bed. Becky looks pretty bad today. She's this awful yellowish shade that makes her look like she's been coloured in with the wrong crayon. She's got needles sticking out of her arms and machines all around her. The worst thing is, I'm getting used to seeing her like this.

'No, I didn't,' I say.

'OK, she didn't,' says Tara. Then she bends over and whispers to Becky. 'Yes, she did.'

Becky laughs, and it's the first time I've heard her laugh in ages. I don't even care that it's at my expense.

'When was this?' Mum's voice sounds shaky. It always does these days.

'Yesterday,' I tell her. 'After school. You're not angry, are you?'

Mum clamps her lips together and shakes her head.

'Good,' I say. 'Because it wasn't even a real date.'

'Except it totally was,' says Tara. 'He asked her in a note and everything.'

'Tara!' I say, giving her a whack on the leg.

Mum smiles. Becky smiles. 'Who's the boy?' they both ask at the same time.

'His name is Joel,' I tell them. 'He's Reece's best friend.'

'How cool,' says Becky. 'Best friends dating best friends.'

'That's what I thought,' I said. 'And he's even in Reece's band too. He plays the guitar.'

'And he's really good,' Tara adds.

'What does he look like?' Mum asks.

'Nice,' I say. 'A bit scruffy.'

'I'm sure you can smarten him up,' says Mum.

I roll my eyes at her. I like him scruffy.

'What else?' asks Mum. 'I want to know everything.'

'When did you become so nosey?' I ask. That's the best thing about my parents – they pretty much let me just get on with my life.

'I just . . . I feel bad,' says Mum. 'I haven't been at home much recently. I should've known about your very first date.'

'I feel bad too,' says Becky.

All three of us reach for Becky's hand, but me and Mum get there first. Tara just manages to grab a finger.

'It's not your fault,' I tell her.

'Doesn't stop me feeling bad about it,' she says.

There are a few things about being Becky it's hard to understand.

Mum's eyes are wet but she pretends she's

not crying. 'So . . . tell me now,' she says. 'How did the date go?'

'Mum!' I am not having this conversation with my mother. 'I told you: it wasn't a date. Gerry was there.'

'Gerry?' asks Mum.

'You know – Gerry,' I say. 'The girl I met on holiday.'

'What was she doing there?' says Mum.

'Good question,' Tara mutters under her breath. 'She totally muscled in on Abby's hot date.'

Mum looks confused, and so does Becky.

'Don't be mean,' I say. 'She's going through a tough time.'

'That's no excuse to ruin someone's date though, is it?' says Becky. Sometimes she sounds twenty-five rather than seven.

'It was good having her there actually,' I say. 'Took the pressure off. It meant we could all talk about the movie together afterwards.'

Tara and Becky shake their heads at each other. 'You know what they call it in engineering terms,' says Tara. 'Third wheel.'

I don't know why I'm defending Gerry. It

was good to have her there at Starbucks. Joel was obviously surprised she came along, but Gerry shrugged off her misery and was her normal funny, crazy self. There were exactly zero awkward silences. She made a hat out of napkins and wore it on her head the whole time, making Joel laugh. Turns out she even supports the same football team as him – Tottenham Hotspur   so they had loads to talk about.

Joel and I didn't do much talking.

And I guess it was my fault that I didn't make it clear to Gerry I wanted to have the cinema part just me and Joel. She came along too. I thought it was a bit weird how she ended up sitting next to Joel rather than next to me. She kept reaching over and stealing his popcorn, giggling every time he got annoyed with her.

And afterwards we did talk about the movie. But it seemed Gerry and Joel both liked it more than I did.

'It was fine,' I say.

'Have you got a second date planned?' asks Mum.

'No,' I say. 'And seeing as this wasn't even

a first date . . .' Truth is, I'm really hoping that didn't count as a first date, because if it *was* a first date, it was kind of rubbish.

'Well, if you do,' says Mum, 'make sure you tell me. I'd love to help you prepare.'

I guess Mum misses doing the normal mother—daughter stuff as much as I do.

Tara looks at her watch. 'I have to go,' she says. 'Loads of homework.' She kisses Becky on the head. 'See you soon, Bexy. Stay sexy.'

Becky giggles. 'Bye, Tara.'

'Go on,' Mum says to me. 'You go too.'

'I'm sure Mr Raza won't mind if I skip this homework,' I say. But it's an old trick and Mum never falls for it.

'Well, I do,' she says. 'Go home. Your father will be there soon to make dinner.'

I give Mum and Becky a kiss each and head out the door. Tara takes my hand. 'You OK?' she says.

I nod. But there is something I need her here for. 'You know that thing I asked you to do . . . ?' I say.

'Want to do it now?'

184

I nod.

Tara and I search the ward. We stick our head into every room and eventually find Adrian making himself a cup of tea in the nurses' station.

'Hey, slacker,' I say to him.

He turns around, and when he sees it's me and Tara he smiles. 'I've been on my feet since six o'clock this morning,' he says. 'What have *you* done today?'

'Triple art was pretty hardcore,' I joke.

He smiles. But my face falls as my mind turns to the question I have been putting off for ages. It's time I stepped up and helped my sister.

'What's wrong?' he asks, picking up on my look.

'I was wondering . . .' I say. I'm not sure if I can finish it. Tara gives my hand a squeeze and I go on. 'I want a blood test. Please.'

'Abby . . .' he starts.

'Please, Adrian,' I say. 'I want to know what blood type I am.'

'Why?' he asks. But he knows why. My sister needs a kidney. And here I am asking what my blood type is.

'Abby,' he says, 'if your parents wanted you to do this they would have already asked.'

'It's my body,' I say. 'Can't I do what I want with it?'

'Not at your age,' says Adrian. 'Sorry.'

Tara steps forward. 'She's not asking you to yank out her kidney right here, right now,' she says, in a little more graphic detail than I wanted. 'She's just asking for a blood test.'

He sighs and rubs his head. 'I could get in trouble . . .'

I start rolling up my right sleeve, to get the process going. 'Just do the test and we'll see what happens.'

Adrian looks up and down the hall. 'Shouldn't we check with your mum?' he asks.

'I want to give my sister a kidney.' The Becky Lump is back and it's huge. I do everything I can to stop my voice from shaking. 'If you can't do this, then I can't save her life. Please.'

Adrian sighs and rubs the back of his head. 'Oh my God.'

'You'll do it?' I ask.

'No.' He holds up his hand when he sees I'm

about to start pleading again. 'But I will look into your records and see what I can find out about your blood type.'

'And if I'm the same blood group as her, I can give her my kidney, right?' I ask.

He shakes his head. 'It's not as simple as that. There are lots of other things to take into consideration – antigens and protein matches, your health. And most of all . . . parental consent.'

That will be the most difficult of all.

'We'll cross that bridge when we come to it,' I tell him.

'Fine,' he says. 'I could still get in trouble. So if anyone finds out, we'll say you caught me when I was sleep-deprived, near mad with tiredness, and desperate for the approval of two glamorous gals.'

'So we'll tell the truth?' asks Tara.

'Yes,' he says.

'Thanks, Adrian,' I say. I know he's doing a lot for me. 'You don't know how much I appreciate it.'

He doesn't say anything as he walks down the corridor.

Tara holds my hand. 'And you say you're not brave,' she says.

Right now I'm wondering what Adrian's going to find out about me on the hospital system. The next part – the part about giving my kidney away – I'm not focusing on that right now. That would require bravery, and I'm not sure I have enough of it.

Chapter 18

'Come on, Lenny!' Donna shouts.

Lenny is dribbling down the pitch – and by *pitch* I mean the space between the two Portakabin classrooms – getting nearer to the goal – and by *goal* I mean the bags that are piled up ten paces apart. We're in the playground at lunchtime. We're supposed to be watching Reece and the boys playing football – an epic grudge match between class 8a and class 8b – but it's far too cold to be enjoyable.

Lenny shoots. Ollie Calder dives but doesn't even get a finger on it.

We all start clapping and whooping.

'Well done, Lenny!' Donna shouts the loudest. 'He's so great, isn't he?' she says to us.

'Do you think he'll dedicate that goal to you?' Sonia asks her.

'He can't dedicate *all* his goals to her,' says Maxie.

We're all sick of hearing how much Lenny does for Donna. Apparently, he's the 'best boyfriend ever'. . . even though neither of them has yet changed their status from 'single' to 'in a relationship'.

They're bringing the ball back to the centre spot when Mrs Martin sticks her head around the corner. Game over.

'Boys! You know you're not allowed to play down here!' she yells.

'Awww, miss,' is the general groan coming from the boys.

'You'll have to wait until after school and head down to the field.'

The boys start gathering up their coats and bags.

I pick up my own bag from the floor. 'Thank God,' I say. 'I'm freezing.'

Reece comes over to us, followed by Lenny and Joel.

I smile at Joel. We haven't spoken since our date and I want to make sure things are OK with us. Trouble is, I have no idea what to say. 'Good match?' I ask him.

He shrugs. 'It wasn't much of a match,' he says. 'We only got ten minutes in.'

'Wouldn't happen at White Hart Lane,' I tell him.

He raises his eyebrows at me. 'What do you know about White Hart Lane?'

'It was built in 1899,' I tell him, 'and has a capacity of 36,240.'

Joel laughs. 'Thank God for Google, eh?'

'You caught me!' I memorized some facts about Joel's favourite team. He and Gerry spoke about it loads and it seemed so easy. I was a bit left out.

'Move a little more quickly, please, children,' Mrs Martin says. 'The open day is just about to start.'

The teachers have been stressy about open day all week. Everything has to be clean. No mess. We've got all this fun computer stuff planned for our classes. The teachers are pretending like we do interesting lessons every day, just to show off.

'We need to showcase the school in its most positive light,' Mrs Martin says.

'You mean, *lie*,' mutters Craig Baker.

Mrs Martin purses her lips. 'If there weren't adults coming into the school I would give you a clip round the ear for that.'

'So I can say whatever I like,' asks Reece, 'like . . . *bum* – and we can get away with it?'

'Go on,' says Mrs Martin with an indulgent smile, 'act like the little devils you are. Personally I would be happy to have no new students.'

'What do you reckon?' says Tara to me. 'Do you think it would be good to have more girls in the school?'

'Definitely,' I say. 'It's been the ten of us against about a thousand of them since the start of term. Would be great to even up the odds.'

Donna wrinkles her nose and Sonia copies her. 'It depends . . . on what kind of girls,' she says.

Tara leans over and whispers to me. 'She wouldn't want anyone interfering in her completely solid relationship with Lenny now, would she?'

I laugh. But then I stop myself. Her completely solid relationship is far more solid than mine and Joel's. I turn to him now.

'What do you think, Joel? Would you like it if more girls signed up to the school?'

But Joel isn't looking at me; he's squinting into the distance. There's a mass of people milling around the gate – prospective students and their parents coming to take a look. Mr McAdam is talking to them.

'Gerry!' Joel shouts.

Everyone looks at him, then follows his gaze to the gate.

It can't be. Surely Gerry would have said if she was coming?

'Oh my God!' says Donna, trying to wrestle some of the attention back. 'Gerry! Babe!' she shouts out to her.

Gerry hears her. Everyone hears her. I'm not sure this is what Mrs Martin meant when she said we should be on our best behaviour. Gerry gives a huge wave.

Hannah looks unsure. 'Is Gerry enrolling at Hillcrest?'

They look at me for an answer.

Donna rolls her eyes. 'Well, duh. Obviously. Otherwise why would her parents have brought her here today?'

Tara's looking at me too.

'She never told me,' I say, mainly to Tara. Then I realize I need to wave back to Gerry, so I do. But not quite as manically as she's waving at me.

'Is she wearing your Paul's Boutique coat?' asks Sonia.

'Umm . . .' She is. It's like she's bought everything she's ever seen me wear. This is starting to get weird.

Obi mutters something to Indiana — I'm not sure but I think it was, 'Keep hold of your wallet.'

By now, Joel has got to Gerry. It kills me the way they're so happy to see each other. I'm too far away to hear, but whatever they're talking about, Gerry is laughing. We catch up to them.

'It would be kind of brilliant to have another Spurs supporter here,' he's saying.

'Yeah,' she says, looking into his eyes. 'I'm surrounded by Gooners at my school.' They both pull the exact same disgusted face.

'Gerry!' I say, trying to make my voice sound enthusiastic. 'What are you doing here?'

'Lovely to see you too!' she says, her mouth open in mock outrage. 'Pleased to see me?'

I guess I'm pleased she's here. She's my friend after all. But if that's true, why do I also feel scared?

'Yeah!' I say. Then I remember I have back-up: the other girls are friends with her now too. 'Aren't we, girls?'

Donna's smiling so Sonia's smiling too – Donna loves that we have attention from the whole playground and the new parents. And I think she'd quite like another wild girl to be loud with . . . as long as it doesn't take the focus off her. Candy and Hannah look unsure – the last time they saw Gerry she was running off with that poor couple's money. Indiana is frowning, probably remembering how she had to deal with the fallout. Obi has crossed her arms and is glaring at Gerry – she couldn't be less welcoming if she tried. Maxie hasn't met Gerry yet, but I'm sure she's heard enough about her to be wary.

Then there's Tara, looking nervous and shy . . . which is so unlike her.

The silence has gone on for a bit too long.

'Oh my God, yes,' says Sonia. 'There's only ten of us girls in the whole school – and that's if you include Simone, who's practically a hermit – so we definitely need you here.'

'Us boys aren't so bad, are we?' asks Lenny.

'You're terrible!' says Gerry, and she laughs. 'If Joel's representative of your school.'

'Hey!' says Joel.

Lenny steps forward. 'He's not,' he says. 'He's really not.'

Gerry laughs. She and Lenny lock eyes for a little too long and Donna sees it. Donna's face falls. She realizes what this means; another girl is more competition . . . and it looks like Gerry's winning.

'What's all this?' Mrs Martin says, smiling her way through the parents to get to us. 'Do you know each other?' She's trying to sound cheery but I think she's worried we're going to mess up this open afternoon for her.

'Yes,' says Gerry. 'Abby and I met on holiday at half-term. She said what an amazing school this is.'

Mrs Martin beams at me. Great! I'm going to be in her good books for weeks. Once again, I owe Gerry.

'She kept on telling my parents how great it was too.' This is a lie – I've never met Gerry's mum and dad – but Mrs Martin doesn't need to know that. Gerry points out her parents, who are in the massive parent huddle listening to Mr McAdam's welcome speech. I peer over to get a look. Gerry's mum has auburn hair, just a shade darker than Gerry's, and her dad is quite dark – his hair is a very deep brown, almost black, and he has a few freckles across his nose.

'I hope we live up to your expectations,' says Mrs Martin. 'Abby, why don't you and the girls show Gerry round the school. I'll tell Mrs Grabovski you might be a little late for maths.'

Miss maths! This is awesome.

'That's so unfair!' says Reece, and I suppose he has a point.

'See ya, losers,' Obi says to Lenny, and he glares at her. Then they both smile.

We're not waiting around to see if Mrs Martin changes her mind. We head for the main school building. I take Gerry by the left arm. As I do, the sleeve of her coat rides up her arm a little and I see it: the friendship bracelet Tara gave me. Identical to the one Tara's got round her wrist. If Tara sees it . . .

'You're welcome, ladies!' Gerry says as the bell goes and all the boys head off to class. The hallway clears and it's just us left.

Tara steps forward. Has she seen the bracelet? I drop Gerry's arm quickly and subtly nudge her sleeve down to cover it.

'Hi, Gerry,' she says. 'It's so nice to finally meet you.' And then Tara, because she's the best, gives her a big hug. Tara's being so sweet to Gerry. But I always knew she would be. It's Gerry I'm worried about. What if she shows her the bracelet? She's threatened to do it before. I'm hoping it was an empty threat.

Gerry looks a bit awkward about being hugged by this girl she's never met. 'Umm . . .'

I can't take my eyes off Gerry's wrist. But what if Tara sees me staring and follows my eyeline?

'Sorry,' Tara says to Gerry, stepping back and laughing. 'That was a bit full on, wasn't it? It's just that I've heard so much about you and I feel like we're friends already. I'm Tara.' She points to Maxie. 'This is my sister, Maxie.'

Tara's bracelet is on display. Will Gerry see the identical bracelet to the one she's wearing? When we argued on the phone she said there was something else I wouldn't want Tara to see. What could it be?

Maxie raises her hand and her eyebrows as her way of saying hello.

'Maxie and Tara may be sisters, but they aren't very alike,' I say with a laugh. I really want to change the subject. I really want Gerry to leave. This is so bad. If Gerry joins the school then every second of every day will be like this. Or worse, Tara will stop being my friend once she finds out I betrayed her.

'We couldn't come last Saturday,' Tara's saying to Gerry. 'Family thing, you know.'

Gerry nods. 'Yeah . . . of course . . . those family things . . .' She rolls her eyes and Tara does too. 'They're the worst.'

'Tell me about it!' Tara flips her hair with her left hand. I catch a glimpse of the blue string on her wrist and my heart flips too. 'We had to sit at my grandma's for four hours, and she doesn't even have Freeview!'

'Nightmare,' says Gerry.

Tara's hand is back by her side, the bracelet covered again.

'Those family things are awful,' I say, diving in between them, trying to hide the matching bracelets from everyone. I force a laugh. I'm really scared – my heart feels so high in my chest I can practically hear it coming through my mouth.

I try to move Gerry on. 'Careful,' I say. 'Your mum and dad will hear you!'

Gerry shrugs. 'They'll probably be lost somewhere. But that's OK – that way I can spend the rest of the day with you guys. Why don't you bunk off and hang out with me? You're already out of maths. You could make an excuse.'

'I've got geography next,' says Sonia. 'Mr Raza doesn't let us get away with anything.'

'There's always someone who ruins it,' says Donna, giving Sonia an evil stare.

'Hey! What's this?' says Gerry.

She points at the noticeboard.

I wince, terrified in case the bracelet shows itself, but she's pointing with her other hand. It's the poster about the Winter Festival. It's weird, but I find myself moving in front of it, as if I can block it from her view.

'It's nothing,' I say. 'You'd probably think it was stupid.'

'Isn't it the thing you guys were talking about last week?' she asks. 'You were all making those mask thingies.'

'Yeah,' says Maxie. 'We're all going together. Want to come?'

Maxie has the excuse that she hasn't properly met Gerry. By the look on Obi's face, I can see she's almost as unhappy about the invitation as I am.

'I don't know if you'd want to, Gerry,' I say quickly.

Gerry turns to me, the dark expression clouding her face. The one I've begun to dread. 'Don't *you* want me to?'

'Of course I do!' I don't. But what can I say? I sneak another glance at her arm. 'I mean, it's just . . . it's kind of a school thing, you know?'

Gerry shrugs. 'Oh, right.' She's caught me looking, so she looks down at her left wrist too.

Donna butts in. 'But Gerry might be at this school next term,' she says. 'Might as well start getting her acquainted.'

Gerry steps away. 'I might come here, I might not.' Her voice has gone all gravelly. 'I haven't made up my mind.' She struts off down the hall.

Tara grabs Gerry by the arm. This is it. She's spotted the bracelet. I can see it right now. I shut my eyes tight.

'Gerry . . .' Tara says.

Gerry looks down at Tara's hand on her arm. Tara's bracelet is right there. Gerry must see it.

202

My head starts swimming and I feel a little sick.

'I just wanted to say . . . thanks,' says Tara.

I open my eyes. Gerry looks confused. 'For what?'

'Abby said how great you were. And I can see she was right. I know you were really nice when Becky was rushed to hospital. Thank you for looking after her.'

'Oh . . . that's OK,' Gerry says. 'You know, it was nothing.'

'Let's not get all mushy,' I say, stepping forward to try to separate them. 'We have to show—'

'Hang on a second, Abs,' Tara continues. 'It's just . . . for me . . . while everyone worries about Becky – and I do, of course I worry about Becky – but I think that while everyone else worries about Becky, it's kind of my job to worry about Abby.'

'Your *job*?' Obi says.

'Does she pay you?' Donna sneers.

'Hey!' I say. But I'm not bothered about Donna insulting me; that's totally normal. It's what's about to happen that's scaring me. My ears start ringing.

'It's my job,' says Tara, 'to look out for her. You know, because that's what best friends do.'

There it is. Tara's said the words 'best friends', and I see Gerry's reaction. And also the reaction of the girls who were there on Saturday. They all jolt back a bit. Gerry's mouth falls open, only a millimetre, but I see it. Her eyes widen by a millimetre too. Tara hasn't picked up on it, the movement was so tiny, but it's like Gerry's been hit with a poisoned arrow. She's frozen.

'I just wanted to say, you know, thanks for looking after my best friend while she was away.'

Tara grabs her in for another hug, and finally I can let my expression change. This is the worst. I tried to tell Gerry, but she wouldn't hear it.

I look up to see if I've made Gerry cry. She's looking at me. Her face still frozen – pupils massive. Then . . .

'Oh, *you're* Tara!' she says, and the pitch is a tone too high. 'Oh my God, it's so nice to finally meet you! I thought we never would. I've heard so much about you.'

She gives her a squeeze so tight that Tara winces.

'Abby's best friend Tara,' she says. Then she looks at me. 'You're a lucky girl. She's always saying how great you are for not ditching her when you started going out with that boy Reece, wasn't it?'

'Umm . . . yeah.' Tara's voice is a little strangled.

That's a weird thing for Gerry to say. But I know why she's saying it.

She looks me in the eye over Tara's shoulder and mouths, *'Ooooh, Reece. He's so dreamy.'*

Oh my God – the drawing I made of Tara. But it's still in my sketchbook . . . isn't it?

Then Gerry rubs her arm along Tara's back so that her sleeve is revealed. She flashes her friendship bracelet. At me. Her look is so dark that I'm scared. It's a warning, a threat. She has my secret and it's wrapped around her wrist.

I betrayed my wonderful best friend Tara by

telling Gerry she was my best friend. I thought it wouldn't matter, I assumed I would never see her again. But Gerry has the evidence.

Over Tara's shoulder, she looks me right in the eye. I have no idea if it's a look that says, *We're in this together*, or, *I'm going to get you for this.*

Chapter 19

Sorry G, can't make it today after all x x

'That should do it,' I say to Tara. 'Short and sweet.'

Gerry invited me to meet her in London after school. I said yes at the time, but then I realized I didn't want to. I *really* didn't want to. I felt it in the pit of my stomach. She's so clingy – texting and ringing and instagramming me constantly. And enrolling in a school that's miles away from her house, just because I'm here, is a bit much. And . . . if I'm honest, I sort of dread seeing her these days.

'Never explain, never apologize,' says Tara. 'I'm sure I've heard that somewhere.'

'It doesn't sound very nice,' I say.

'It's assertive,' says Tara. 'Stop worrying. Now where's your craft box?' She heads to my cupboard. 'Let's make our masks.' She opens the door and pulls out all the art stuff. Including my pad of paper.

My heart stops.

That's where the mean drawing of Tara is! Why didn't I get rid of it?

I hurry over to help, pulling the pad from her hands so quickly I might have given her paper cuts.

'It's OK,' says Tara, giving me a weird look, 'I can do it.'

I feel hot and faint and I know I'm bright red. If Tara sees that drawing, she'll hate me forever.

She plonks the craft box on the floor and starts getting everything out – glue, glitter, sequins, little knick-knacks, gems and scraps of material – as well as loads of pens and coloured paper. The box is something Mum started for me when Becky was born and I was spending a lot of time entertaining myself in the hospital. I guess I never grew out of it.

While she's doing that, I open the pad of paper, angling it carefully so Tara can't see.

I have to find the picture, tear it out and destroy it. I wish I'd never drawn it in the first place.

'Remember when I went as Little Red Riding Hood to book day in Year 4?' she asks me.

I nod, but I'm not really listening, flipping through the pages of my sketch pad.

'I still have the red cape.'

Where's the drawing? All the other stuff I drew on holiday is here.

'I thought I could wear that with the elf costume. Do you think it would go?'

'Umm . . .' I have to listen to what Tara's saying so she doesn't ask what I'm doing. 'What else are you wearing?' I ask. I stand up, backing away from her so she can't see the pad.

'I have red-and-white stripy tights, a red skirt and a green top.' She cringes a little, unsure. 'And I was going to wear my brown boots.'

'Great,' I assure her. 'I'll wear the same.'

She smiles. Tara is so pretty, with a lovely boyfriend, and yet she *still* needs my approval to feel OK about herself. I guess she's just as insecure as I am, deep down.

I still can't find the picture, so I flip through the pages more carefully, one by one.

'What were you thinking for our masks?' Tara asks me.

'Umm . . . I think they should just cover our eyes.' Luckily I've been planning them for a while.

'Or . . .' says Tara, 'we could do *Phantom of the Opera* style, over one side of our faces.'

I force a laugh to hide the fact my stomach is sinking. I can't find the drawing anywhere. 'I think that's cool,' I say, 'but just eyes and nose is prettier.'

My phone beeps and it makes me jump. Tara laughs at me for flinching.

I tuck the pad under my arm and read the text.

Come on! It will be fun!!!

Gerry. I should have expected it.

I show the screen to Tara. 'What shall I say now?'

She grabs the phone from me. 'How about . . .'

I know it will be fun. You're always fun. I just can't today x x

She presses send.

I bite my lip. I'm cringing inside. I'm not sure Tara gets how persistent Gerry can be.

My phone beeps again:

Why?

Tara frowns as if it's the phone's fault Gerry keeps texting. 'Just ignore it,' she says. 'You don't need to give any more details. Come on! Back to the job in hand: masks!'

I do have a brilliant idea for our masks. 'OK', I say, 'what I was thinking is that we would have little diamonds, and we'd put them on like this.' I kneel down and arrange the diamond studs on the mask so they surround the eyeholes. 'I think it will make our eyes look twinkly.'

'Nice,' Tara says.

'But that's not all,' I say. 'On the night, we stick a few of the jewels to our cheeks so that it looks like they're falling off our masks and on to our faces.'

'Oh my God, that's brilliant!' she says. 'Don't tell the others. Let's do it just us two.'

It's nice to feel like a team again. We've drifted apart since we started Hillcrest and Tara started going out with Reece. But the thing is, we are best friends, always will be. If our masks match and are better than everyone else's, it'll let people know.

I just need Gerry out of my life. And to destroy that drawing. If I could just find it.

'You start on the gluing,' I tell Tara. 'I'm just . . . looking for something.'

'What?'

'Erm . . .' Oh God, I'm going to have to lie again to cover the lie.

Luckily my phone rings so I don't have to say anything.

But *un*luckily, it's Gerry. Of course.

'Seriously?!' Tara mutters. I get the sense Tara is almost as jealous of Gerry as Gerry is of Tara.

All this is my fault. I cringe. 'What should I do?'

'Ignore it,' says Tara. 'I know you feel bad.'

She doesn't know the half of it.

'But imagine what kind of world it would be if we all went round telling the exact truth all the time,' Tara continues. 'You don't want to see her. Much better to make up a fake reason than say, *I don't want to see you*, and hurt her feelings.'

Tara's making sense. And I would prefer to say *I can't* rather than *I won't*. That doesn't make me mean, does it?

'Are you sure?' I ask her.

'If Gerry is a normal person, she'll take the hint without you having to be rude. Come on, how many times do you have to say, *Thanks but no thanks*, before she gets it?'

It *is* my fault for lying . . . but could Tara be right? Is it a little bit Gerry's fault for not picking up on the hints?

My phone stops ringing.

Then it starts again.

Gerry. *Again*.

Tara gives a proper huff now. 'Just make

something up,' she says, and hands me my phone.

'Hello,' I say to Gerry. 'Sorry I can't come today. How are you?'

'Ab-bee!' Gerry whines. 'Please come. It's been ages since me and you hung out.'

'I saw you yesterday, when you came to my school, remember?' *When you turned up out of the blue and threatened me over my best friend's shoulder.*

Tara rolls her eyes.

'But that was hardly hanging out, was it?' Gerry says. 'I don't know about you, but my idea of fun involves us being as far away from school as possible.'

'I know, but . . .' Why is Gerry being so needy?

'We can have a really cool time. We could go to the Trocadero, play some arcade games.' There's a desperation in her voice that makes me scared. Like she's trying too hard to make it sound exciting. But it doesn't sound exciting, it sounds suffocating. 'I'll see if I can pick up a replacement Mack.'

With anyone else I'd be tempted to go. But not with Gerry.

'And we could also pick up any other stuff we need.'

'Sorry, Gerry,' I say, and Tara frowns at me for apologizing. 'Can't afford it.'

'You know that isn't a problem for us.' I hear mischief in her voice, and now I'm even less tempted. I think I know what she means, and if it's stealing, I don't want to be involved.

'Not today,' I say.

'But *why*?' She's starting to sound like a clingy toddler. I feel my throat tightening like she's strangling me.

Tara nods at me and mouths, '*Do it.*'

I trot out my fail-safe excuse that always works. 'I have to go and see Becky.'

'Oh . . . OK then. Of course. Sorry.'

Tara gives me a thumbs-up with an eyebrow question mark attached. I give her a thumbs-up back. Job done.

'Is Becky OK?' Gerry asks.

'She's . . . OK.' I hesitate over the OK so it

could mean anything; it could mean she's fine, or that she's not OK at all.

'So is she better or worse?' God, this girl knows how to pester.

'I don't know. She's a little worse, I think.' I cringe at Tara, who winces at my lie.

'Oh my God!' says Gerry. 'You better get down to the hospital right now!'

'Er . . . yeah. Thanks Gerry,' I say. 'And sorry about today.'

Tara frowns deeper.

'Don't be ridiculous!' Gerry says. 'Do you need me to do anything?'

'No, thanks,' I say. 'But thanks.'

'If there is anything I can do, you know I'll do it, don't you?'

'Thanks, Gerry. I have to go.'

'*Anything*,' she says again.

I get the message: she'll do *anything* for me. But why, if she's meaning to be nice, does it just terrify me more?

'OK. Thanks. Got to go. Bye.' I hang up on her, then hang my head. There's a chance I might be the worst person in the world.

'Wow!' says Tara. 'Will that girl ever give up?'

I exhale a long breath. I hated that. But at least it's done.

'I said you should lie,' Tara says, 'but I didn't say you should lie about your sister.'

I sigh. 'I know it's bad. But Becky's cool with it,' I say. 'In fact, it was her idea in the first place. She said if she had to be ill, there should at least be some advantages. She ordered me to use it as my *Get Out of Jail Free* pass for homework or anything, whenever I wanted.'

'Your sister's the best,' says Tara. She picks her mask back up and says, 'I'm going to start gluing, OK?'

I nod. But I do feel guilty. 'After this, let's go to the hospital.'

Tara laughs at me. 'That's what I love about you, Abs,' she says. 'You are *so* not cut out for a life of crime.'

I laugh too. I wonder if I will have to use Becky as an excuse every time I need to lie to Gerry. How long will it take for her to leave me alone?

I go back to searching for the picture. In the place where I know it should be, I see a page has been ripped out.

Oh God. Please don't let this mean what I think it does. If Gerry has the picture of Tara, who knows what she'll do with it?

Chapter 20

I round the corner of the long hospital corridor.
I've brought Becky a book from the library.

Mum and Dad outside her room, talking to
Dr Hayward. At first my stomach flips – what's
wrong? Has Becky got worse? But then Dad
smiles. Mum even laughs.

'Mum?' I call down the corridor.

Mum turns and beams at me. 'Hello,
darling!' she says.

'Good news?' I ask.

'Good news,' says Dad, holding his arms out
for a hug. I run into him and he wraps them
round me. 'Becky's doing much better. She can
come home!'

'Really?'

'Today,' says Dr Hayward.

'That's brilliant!' I say.

We hug again. When I pull back, I look in

at Becky. And then I see who's sitting by her bedside.

'Your friend is in there with her,' says Dad.

Gerry.

Oh God. Gerry's reading to Becky from one of her comics, showing her the pictures as she read the words out. What the hell is she doing here?!

'She's such a nice girl,' says Mum.

She wouldn't say that if she had any idea what Gerry was really like. I didn't ask her to come to the hospital. I don't want her here. Is it me, or it is really weird that she's come?

I leave the adults talking and head into the room to confront her.

'Hi, Abby!' Becky calls. 'Did you hear? They said I can go home.'

She sounds so happy, but I'm looking at Gerry. The dark expression clouding her face. The big pupils. She's angry.

I give her a look that I hope she knows says, *I'm sorry I lied, but . . .*

But what? The reason I lied is that I find her too needy and intense. I'm starting to

220

think it's not me who's in the wrong here.

Finally I look at Becky. She's smiling from ear to ear. I smile back at her. She's coming home. My family will be together again.

'Isn't that great, Abby?' says Gerry, and it's easy to detect the sneer in her voice. 'I've been so worried about Becky. She was so ill. I raced over here to see her.' She narrows her eyes at me. 'Such a *pleasant surprise* to hear the good news.' Her voice is gravelly.

I do feel sorry for Gerry, but then I feel sorry for myself again. The day my sister gets out of hospital is supposed to be a good day. But Gerry's here. And somehow it's all about her again.

'You big faker,' says Gerry, smiling at Becky.

Becky laughs.

I kiss Becky on the head. 'Sleepover in your room tonight?'

Becky nods. 'Yeah!'

'I'll ask Mum if she'll let us watch a movie.'

'I'll ask if she'll let us eat some diabetic chocolates.'

Becky has to watch her sugar intake because

of her kidney problem. She's occasionally allowed to eat diabetic chocolates. But they aren't actually very nice.

'Wish I could go to a sleepover party,' Gerry whines.

'Why don't you join us?!' Becky says, and my heart sinks.

'I doubt Mum will go for it,' I say, a little too quickly. 'Not tonight.' I stage-whisper to Gerry, 'Besides, Becky's no fun, she's usually snoring before we've popped the popcorn.'

'Spoilsport,' Gerry gestures at me.

'That's what big sisters do,' says Becky. 'Spoil the fun.'

'Maybe another time, yeah?' I say to them both. But by the time another time comes around, I'm hoping Gerry will have forgotten I mentioned it.

I can't sit around and wait for Gerry to disappear. I have to ask her to back off a little. Or even a lot.

'Gerry,' I say, 'can I have a word outside?'

'Uh-oh,' Gerry says to Becky. 'Sounds like trouble.'

'You're not in trouble!' I say, and laugh too hard.

'Then why can't you say it in front of Becky? Is it a boyfriend thing? I'm sure Becky can take it. She seems very wise for an eleven-year-old.'

'I'm seven!' says Becky.

'Wow, I thought you were so much older.'

Becky beams.

It's like Gerry's doing this on purpose. I'm trying to be sympathetic, but it's very frustrating. 'Can you just come outside?'

Gerry and Becky exchange a look, like *they* are the friends and I'm the one who's barging in.

There's a coffee machine down the hallway and I drag Gerry there. 'I need to speak to you,' I say.

'No kidding,' says Gerry, her eyes fiery with anger. 'I raced down here because you said Becky was worse. I can't believe you'd use your own sister's health—'

'Hi, girls. Great news about Becky, eh?'

I turn. It's Adrian. I have to stop myself from rolling my eyes. Not because I don't want to see him, but because I was just getting up

223

the nerve to speak to Gerry and he's spoiled it.

'Hi, Adrian,' I say. 'Yeah, it's great.'

I turn away from him and back to Gerry. I don't want to be rude but . . .

'Actually, Abby,' he says, 'I was wondering if I could have a quick word.'

I clench my teeth, then turn to Adrian.

'You know how to amuse yourself, don't you, Gezza?' he says to Gerry. *Gezza?* Since when are these two so pally?

He leads me a few steps into the nurses' office. 'I just wanted to let you know what I found out.'

Even with everything that's going on, my stomach flips. Here we go.

'I'm really sorry, Abby,' he says.

What does that mean? Is he's sorry because I can't give my sister my kidney or sorry that I can?

'I'm afraid you aren't a suitable match,' he says.

I feel like I'm falling. I lean against the wall so I don't actually faint.

'You can't donate your kidney to Becky,' he adds, even though it was clear the first time.

'But . . . I don't understand . . . I'm her sister.'

'I'm afraid that doesn't make it a certainty,' he tells me.

'Oh.'

'How are you feeling?' he says.

'Um . . .' and I really don't know. I guess this thing was always a lose-lose situation – I either lose a kidney or risk losing my sister. I guess that's why Mum and Dad didn't want me tested. The Becky Lump is back and it finally bursts. I start to cry.

'I'm really sorry, Abby,' he says.

Thing is, I'm not sure that I am. If I was a match, would I have been willing to give her my kidney? Have an operation? Live the rest of my life in fear of getting sick?

I gulp for breath. 'Thanks,' I say, struggling to get the words out. 'For doing that for me.'

Adrian puts his hand on my shoulder. 'No problem,' he says. 'You're a good sister, you know.'

He's only saying that because he doesn't know how relieved I am. I'm such a bad person. A terrible sister. I cry harder.

When I look up I see that he's motioning to someone behind me, waving them in. Good. I really need a hug from Mum right now. She might be angry with me for doing this, but—

I look and see it's Gerry. She's been listening in this whole time! Has she got no boundaries?

'Come on, Gezza, your friend needs you,' he says, smiling at Gerry, then looking over to me with pity as he goes off down the corridor.

I do need a friend, but not Gerry.

'Oh, Abby,' says Gerry. She runs forward and gives me a big hug. I'm cringing. 'I'm so sorry. You must be so upset. You really wanted to give Becky your kidney. That was the one thing you could do for her. And now . . .'

That's not how I'm feeling. Or at least, it's only part of it. Tara would understand. I push out of the hug.

'I'm sorry, Gerry,' I say, giving her a weak smile. 'I need to be by myself for a bit.'

Gerry looks hurt. She clenches her jaw and

her face does its darkening thing. But she tries to hide it by nodding and looking all sympathetic. 'Of course, of course,' she says.

She backs away and instantly I'm able to breathe a little easier.

'I'll go wait with Becky,' Gerry says. 'Maybe your Mum will let me sleep over after all. If you tell her you're upset. We could stuff our faces full of Aeros.'

My face falls and I can't hide it.

'No,' I say. 'Can you just leave?'

She flinches like I've just punched her. I feel like a horrible person, but maybe it's like Tara said – maybe Gerry's not that great if she won't give me space when I need it.

'Oh,' she says. 'OK. Fine. It's like that, is it?'

She turns. She brings her hand up to her face so I can't see her expression.

'I'm sorry, Gerry. I just . . . I should be with my family right now.'

Gerry starts to sniff. She's crying.

'Gerry . . .'

She flicks her head up and looks me in the

eye. Weirdly, she doesn't look that upset. She looks really, really angry. The darkness in her expression has filled with hatred and her eyes are narrow. 'Why did you lie about Becky being sick today?'

I sigh. 'I need a little distance from you.'

'But why lie about it? If you'd have said that, I would have understood.'

'Would you though?' I say.

Her mouth drops open, outraged. 'What do you mean?!'

'You're so . . . demanding,' I tell her, and saying it is easier than I expected. 'You won't accept no for an answer. I felt I had to lie or else you wouldn't stop bugging me.'

'I *bug* you?' Her lower lip starts to wobble.

'No . . .' I say. 'It's just . . .' I guess I sort of am saying that.

'This is not how you are supposed to treat your best friend, you know, Abby.'

I inhale deeply. 'You are not my best friend, Gerry.'

She makes a little squeaking noise like I have stolen her breath.

'I should never have said you were,' I say.

'But . . . you gave me your friendship bracelet,' she says.

That's not exactly what happened. 'No,' I say, 'you took it. And I shouldn't have let you. That's the bracelet Tara gave me.'

Gerry looks confused, but I don't know why. Surely it must be clear by now.

'Tara is my best friend, Gerry,' I say. 'Always has been. Always will be. My best friend forever.'

Tears brim in Gerry's eyes and spill down her cheeks. She covers her mouth with her hand.

'I'm sorry, Gerry,' I tell her. 'I shouldn't have misled you. I really like you and I should have told you—'

Gerry raises her hand to stop me from speaking. No, that's not what she's doing. She's getting something from her inside pocket. 'Tara's your best friend?' she sneers. 'You sure have a funny way of showing it.'

She pulls out a folded-up piece of paper. I recognize the quality and the colouring. And the rip at the top.

'What's that?' I ask her.

She smirks. 'I think you know,' she says. She puts it back in her pocket. And I do know: it's the mean drawing of Tara.

When did she take it? While we were away on holiday? *Why* did she take it? Did she think she'd need a hold over me, even back then?

'Give it to me,' I tell her.

Gerry shakes her head. 'Nope. It might come in useful.'

'What are you going to do?' I ask. My voice is shaking. She has the thing that could ruin my friendship with Tara forever.

Gerry shrugs. And smiles. It's the evilest smile I've ever seen. 'Haven't decided yet,' she says. 'But you be nice to me and I'll be nice to you. That's what friends do, right?'

I can't speak. I can't believe she's blackmailing me to be her friend.

'Right?' she growls.

'Right,' I whisper.

Gerry smiles again. But this time, the darkness is gone. 'Cool,' she says, like everything that just happened was normal.

This girl is seriously deranged. I'm filled with dread.

'So let me know about when you want to do the sleepover,' she says. 'And let's definitely do the Trocadero some time soon. Yeah?'

'Um. Yeah,' I whisper.

'Byeeee!' she squeals, then she turns and runs out of the room.

I have had such huge news today – first that my sister is well enough to come home. Then, that I can't do anything to cure my sister's long-term health problems, even if I wanted to. But somehow, Gerry threatening me means I can't focus on all that.

Now she has this hold over me, how will I ever get her out of my life?

Chapter 21

Hi hun. When we having that sleepover at yours? x x

Gerry.

The girls and I are in the dining room at lunch. They're talking about how their costumes are coming on, but I'm not really listening.

'I *was* going to wear this long green elf hat, with a cute bell on it,' Donna's saying, 'but I think Lenny would prefer it if I was showing more of my face, you know?'

That's the twenty-ninth text Gerry's sent since Saturday. I don't want to reply, but if I leave it longer than five minutes she sends another. And another.

Soon. Promise. Just let me ask my mum x x

'And your hair,' says Sonia. 'You'll want him to see your hair – that's your best feature.'

'That's *one* of my best features,' says Donna. Another text from Gerry:

I'm holding you to that promise. Sleepover soon, or else ☺ *x x*

The smiley face doesn't dilute the threat.

Of course. As soon as possible.

My phone beeps again straight away. I hate that noise now. I don't have to look to know it's her. It's always her. But what can I do? I have to pretend to like her just to keep her from saying anything to Tara.

Tara nudges me and I jump. She rolls her eyes at Donna. 'Doubt she could find an elf hat big enough to fit over her gigantic head,' she whispers, giggling.

'Who?' I ask.

'Er . . . earth to Abby,' says Tara. 'What's with you today? I thought you'd be happy that Bex is home – instead you've been a right misery guts.'

'Don't be so mean, Tara,' Indiana says. 'How are you doing, Abby?'

'I'm fine, thanks,' I say.

They're all looking at me as if Becky has gotten sicker, not better.

'Are you texting, Joel?' asks Candy.

'Um . . . no,' I say. Why would I be texting Joel? 'Gerry.'

They all nod as if they were expecting me to say that.

'Did she apologize?' asks Maxie.

Weird. Do they know about Gerry black-mailing me?

'Let her have it, Abs,' says Obi. 'She should be more loyal than that.'

Tara looks as clueless as I am.

'I'm just saying hi,' I tell them. 'She wants to stay the night.'

'Why the hell would you let her?' says Obi, frowning deeply, her eyebrows like ski slopes.

When I look around the group they are all doing the same.

'What are you talking about?' asks Tara.

'Have you not seen Facebook?' asks Candy, who checks it almost every second.

I shake my head. 'I've been with my sister.'

'Seen what on Facebook?' asks Tara.

Donna whispers to Sonia, 'Tara's not friends with Gerry, is she?'

From the looks on all their faces, whatever they are about to say is going to be bad. Even the word *Gerry* makes me nauseous these days.

I get Facebook up on my phone.

'Gerry checked in at the cinema yesterday,' says Maxie.

'On a date,' says Hannah.

I finally get on to Gerry's Facebook page. And there it is. She checked in at the Imax in Waterloo.

'With Joel,' finishes Donna.

Watching the new alien attack movie. Can't wait — with Joel Owens

That little cow!

Tara's reading it over my shoulder. She leans

her head on me. 'I'm sorry, Abby,' she says. 'That's lame.'

Blackmailing me was just the beginning – now she's after Joel. I bet she's not doing it because she likes him, only to get back at me.

But either way, Joel went on the date. That means he likes her.

I blow out all the air in my lungs. I've cried too many times in school and I don't want to do it again.

'Did she tell you she fancied him?' Maxie asks me.

I shake my head. 'But they seemed to have loads to talk about. Who knows?'

Maybe I'm being too harsh on Gerry. No one could be that psycho, could they?

But while I'm looking at it, Gerry's page updates with a new status:

Did you know that Abby Gardner used to be really really disgustingly fat?

Now I *know* she's out to get me. And because she has that picture, there's nothing I can do about it.

Chapter 22

It's after school and Tara, Maxie, Obi and me are in the shopping centre, heading over to Starbucks.

'It's been ages since we've played Gorgeous Boy Safari,' says Tara, making binoculars out of her fingers and looking down at the floor below.

'Probably because you're going out with Reece now,' says Maxie. 'You've ensnared your prey . . .'

Tara laughs. 'Just because you see a giraffe on safari doesn't mean you don't want to catch a glimpse of a rhino or two.'

I try to laugh, but I'm not in the mood. Gerry has posted more status updates about me being fat. The other Boys' School Girls have written comments underneath, telling Gerry she's out of order, but she hasn't taken her posts down.

I've texted her to ask her to stop. She just replied:

So NOW you reply to my texts! Not so easy to ignore me any more, is it?

I want to tell someone but I can't. If I do anything she doesn't like, Gerry might post the picture of Tara.

We finally get to Starbucks. Donna and Sonia are there.

'Hey, ladies!' Tara calls to them. 'Can we pull up a chair?'

Donna gives us a dirty look, but this is nothing new, so we sit down anyway.

'What do you fancy, Abby?' says Tara. 'My treat, to celebrate Becky getting out of hospital.'

'Thanks, Tara,' I say. 'A latte please.'

'What would you fancy, Tara?' says Donna, and she sounds annoyed. 'Oh yeah, I forgot: you want everything.'

Tara and I exchange looks. This is classic Donna. Not worth worrying about.

'I'll get the coffees,' Tara says, rolling her eyes and walking away with Obi.

'Cow,' Donna says under her breath. Sonia sniggers.

'Hey!' says Maxie. 'That's my sister you're insulting.'

Donna blushes a little.

'You've always had a problem with Tara,' I say. 'Why don't you drop it?'

'I haven't always had a problem with Tara . . .' Her voice is light and breezy, then it deepens. 'But now I have a *big* one.'

I squint at her. Part of me wants to get up and leave. Part of me wants to wipe the stupid look from her face. 'What's she done now? Has someone said she has nicer hair than you?'

'Has she bought the top you wanted?' asks Maxie, joining in.

Although actually, after having experienced it with Gerry, I know how creepy it is when someone copies all the clothes you wear.

'This is much more serious than that,' says Sonia. 'Tara's been cheating on Reece.'

Maxie laughs. 'Don't be ridiculous.'

It's *so* ridiculous I laugh too. 'Where did you get that from?'

'Facebook,' says Donna. 'Gerry must have found out from Joel or something.'

As soon as she says Gerry's name my heart rises up and fills my throat. It's like when I think about Becky being ill . . . It's the Becky Lump – the same sort of fear, but this time it's more like dread: the Gerry Dread.

'What's she done now?' I ask.

Tara and Obi come over with the drinks. 'Someone take this from me, please, quick, it's burning my . . .' She stops when she sees the way we're all looking at her. 'What?' She puts down the coffees and starts smoothing her hair. '*What?*'

'Whatever, Tara,' says Donna. 'Stop acting all nice. Your secret's out!'

'What secret?' asks Obi, grinning. 'Because everyone knows about Tara's teddy bear, Mr Snuggles-Huggles.' Her face falls when she sees no one laughing.

I pick up my phone and go straight to Gerry's Facebook page.

'It's Reece I feel sorry for,' says Donna.

'He must be heartbroken,' says Sonia. 'His girlfriend and one of his best friends.'

'Just spit it out, won't you?' says Obi.

I get to Gerry's page. It's still loaded on my screen from last time I checked, with all the posts saying: *'Abby Gardner is a fat cow'* over and over again. But then the page updates. I see five new posts, and all of them read:

Tara Simmons is a slag

Tara's not tagged. They aren't friends on Facebook.

Tara Simmons is cheating on her boyfriend with Lenny.
She is a massive slag.

There are loads of comments below.

Is this true?
How do you know?
Really? Does Reece know?

Gerry has replied:

I have my ways. But yes, 100% true.

I show my phone to Tara. Her mouth drops open as she reads it. 'What the . . . ? Why would Gerry say that?' She looks up at me. 'I've never done anything to her. I hardly even know her.'

Gerry is taking it to a new level – blackmail, revenge, and now attack – and it's got vicious.

'She has no reason to lie,' says Donna. 'Therefore, it's obviously true.'

'It's not!' Tara protests.

'Of course it's not,' says Obi. 'Lenny wouldn't do that either.'

'You are such a liar,' Donna says to Tara. 'You have always been a jealous—'

But Tara cuts her off. 'Oh God.' Her eyes widen. She goes completely pale. 'Do you think Reece has seen this?' She gets her phone out and taps at it. 'Reece?' she says.

I can't hear what he's saying back to her, but it doesn't sound like he's saying much.

'Did you see this thing on—' she starts to

say, but he cuts her off. 'It's not!' she says. 'Ask Lenny!'

More from Reece. Tara gets up and starts walking away from the table so she can talk in private.

I feel so awful. If I come clean to everyone, I can clear this whole mess up. But then Gerry will reveal the picture. I will have to tell Tara the truth about what I did – the picture, the bracelet, everything. I'm not sure Tara will ever forgive me. I would die if I lost Tara's friendship. I don't know what to do. She's pacing outside on the phone, talking to Reece while sobbing her eyes out.

'It's not true, you know,' I say to the others.

'You *would* stick up for her,' says Donna. 'I can't believe Tara would steal Lenny when she knows how much me and him like each other.'

'She hasn't stolen Lenny!' I say. 'Ask Lenny!'

'OK, I will.' Donna starts texting Lenny. Donna's phone instantly rings. 'It's him,' she says.

I hope Lenny can clear this mess up.

I go onto Instagram and look at Gerry's feed.

It reads: *Tara Simmons is a slag* over and over again. She's posted it every thirty seconds for the last half-hour.

Gerry is seriously messed up in the head. More than I thought. I know I lied to her, but this is an over-the-top reaction, isn't it? Or is this really all my fault?

'Look at this.' I show the others.

'I'll kill her,' says Maxie.

'What the hell is her problem?!' says Obi. 'She's a crazy person.'

Obi's right. Gerry is completely crazy. I've made her crazy.

'You should report her,' says Maxie.

I'm worried about her revealing the truth to Tara. But if Gerry really is crazy, then I have to do something to stop her. The girls are all looking at me. If I don't report Gerry, they'll wonder why.

I try to find how to report Facebook abuse but I can't seem to do it from my phone, I have to do it from a computer. I stand up, I'm going home to do it now.

Outside, Tara's still pacing.

'Please, Reece,' she begs, 'you have to believe me.'

She looks at me, her eyes like deep puddles.

'I'm coming round to talk to you now,' she says.

'Don't bother,' he yells down the phone, loud enough for me to hear.

Tara looks at her phone in disbelief. He must have hung up on her.

I give her a big hug, and I can feel her shaking as she cries.

'Don't worry, Tara,' I say. 'No one really thinks you did this. It'll all get sorted out. Go to Reece's house—'

'He doesn't want to see me!' she wails.

'Go anyway,' I tell her. 'Convince him that it's all a lie.'

'Gerry is such a cow,' she says.

'I know.' I say. 'I'll speak to her. I'll get her to tell the truth. Do you want me to come with you to Reece's?'

Tara shakes her head. 'No, thanks,' she says. She hugs me again. 'But thanks, Abby, I know I can always rely on you.'

I gulp back the guilt.

Tara goes one way and I head off in the other.

I have to make everything OK. I will never forgive myself if Reece dumps Tara over this. I need a plan. First things first – I'll get online and report Gerry's posts and hopefully they'll stop her account. Then I'll go to see Tara and tell her everything, and tell Reece everything too, and apologize. Hopefully they will forgive each other. And if they are feeling really, really kind, maybe they will forgive me too.

Not that I deserve it.

Chapter 23

Gerry's not answering my calls any more.

I've already reported her on Facebook and now I'm on Instagram. They have a form you have to fill in; it's all pretty easy to do. I just wonder if they'll take me seriously.

I have to put in Gerry's username – it's so weird that it's still @AbbysBFF – she is acting nothing like a best friend now.

I link to the posts she's written, calling Tara a slag. It recommends that I block her. Weirdly, this makes me nervous . . . I'd rather know what she's up to.

Then I get back on to Facebook: time to defriend Gerry. I get up on to her page and I see that she's just checked in. In Wimbledon. She's here and she didn't tell me. She must be meeting up with Joel. I can feel my heart wringing itself out.

She's checked in and written.

Catching up with old friends . . .

My phone rings. It's Tara.

'Hi, Tara, how did it go with—'

'Abby!' she shouts, she's panting. 'Abby! Help me!' I can hear the pounding of feet. She's running.

I stand up so quickly my chair falls backwards. 'What's the matter?'

'Someone's chasing me!' she says.

'Are you sure?' My heart starts beating faster than Tara's footsteps. 'Oh my God.'

'I'm in the park, on my way to Reece's, and someone's following me. But every time I turn around, there's no one there.'

'Are you sure?' I ask.

But *I'm* sure. The repeated posts about Tara. The threats. This is Gerry. I know it is. I'm already downstairs and putting my coat on. 'Do you know who it is?'

'No,' she says. Her voice is wobbling. 'I'm really scared.'

It's half past five, so when I open the front door it's dark already.

'I thought it was one of the girls,' she says, 'but . . . why won't they answer when I shout hello? It's not funny.' She's gasping for breath. 'Reece won't answer my calls.'

'I'm coming,' I say. 'Just . . . go somewhere where there are other people, OK?'

''Kay,' she says. 'Please hurry, Abby.'

'Abby!' Mum shouts. 'What are you doing?'

'Going to meet Tara!' I yell. 'Back soon.' I slam the door before she can argue, then race around to the side of the house where my bike is.

I have to stand on tiptoes to reach over the top of the side gate and undo the bolt. It'll take me two minutes to get to Tara. I just hope I can reach her before Gerry does.

I pull my bike round to the front of the house. It feels heavy, odd for some reason. I look down. The tyres are completely flat.

'No!' I say out loud. This is really bad luck.

But then the sinking feeling comes back — the Gerry Dread. This isn't bad luck; what's the probability of getting a puncture in both tyres at the same time?

I pick up the front of my bike and squeeze the tyre. It splits apart. There's a long gash down it.

Gerry has slashed my tyres.

She's done that, then gone stalking Tara – it's like she knows I won't be able to save her. What's she planning to do?

I consider asking Mum for a lift, but she'd have to bring Becky along, there would be too many questions, and I don't think there's time. I run as fast as I can. But I need help. I call Reece.

'Abby,' he says, his voice flat. 'Look, I really don't want to talk—'

'Reece!' I shout. 'This is serious. Tara's in trouble!'

'What?' I've got his attention. He's listening.

'She's on her way to your house—'

'I told her I didn't want to see her,' he growls.

'Reece! Listen!' I say. 'She's being followed.'

'What?' Now he sounds really worried.

'Someone's chasing her,' I tell him. I'm running too now, so he must understand how urgent this is. 'I'm trying to get to her — she's in the park. It might be quicker if you go.'

'OK,' he says, and I can tell he's moving. 'I'm on my way. Call me if you get to her before I do.'

'You too,' I say. 'Now run.'

I hang up the phone and run with it in my hand. It's usually ten minutes to Reece's house from mine, but if I run really fast, maybe I can get there in five.

In the park there's no sign of Tara. No sign of Gerry either, but what does that mean? Surely Gerry's not the kind of person who would beat someone up? I'm half expecting to see Tara's body in a heap on the ground. And I'm starting to wonder — how much do I really know about Gerry? Is she violent?

I'm out the other side of the park and on Tara's street. She lives just round the corner from Reece so it's on the way.

I'm praying she's OK. I would die if—

In the distance I see two people huddled together. Is that Tara and Gerry? What's she doing to her?

'Tara!' I try to shout out, but I'm out of breath so it's not very loud. 'Tara!' I call again.

The bodies pull apart. Tara and Reece. I could collapse with relief.

They look at me, their pale faces shining in the darkness.

I catch up with them. 'Tara, oh my God,' I say, and give her a hug. 'I'm so glad you're OK. Are you OK?'

She nods, but she's still crying. 'Reece got to me just now.' She looks up at him. 'Thank you.'

'It's all right,' he says. He's a mess. I can tell he doesn't know whether to be angry with her or not.

'Reece, I have to tell you something,' I say. This is it. It's time I told them. Whatever happens to me, it's not worth lying any more. 'Tara didn't meet up with Lenny. You know that really, don't you?'

Tara and I look at him. He wants to trust Tara, but he's not sure. 'Then why would Gerry say she did?'

'I don't know,' says Tara, 'but it's not true. I promise.'

'I know why she'd say it,' I tell them. 'Gerry was the person who chased you tonight. Gerry has it in for Tara.'

'Why?' Reece scrunches up his face. Now he's confused. 'What's Tara ever done to her?'

Both sets of eyes are on me. Tara's are watery from crying, twinkling in the darkness.

'It's my fault,' I tell them.

Tara steps a little closer to Reece.

'How do you work that one out?' Reece says.

'She's jealous of you,' I tell her.

'Why?' she says. 'I've only met her once.'

I take a deep breath. 'When I was on holiday . . .' I can't believe I am about to say it. 'When me and Gerry were on holiday this half-term —' I am about to lose Tara forever — 'I told her she was my best friend.'

Tara bites her lip.

'I only said it because she said I was her best friend. She was being so nice. I didn't think it was a big deal.'

Tara nods slowly. The sides of her mouth are pulling downwards.

'I didn't think I would ever see her again, so I thought it wouldn't matter.'

'Nice,' says Tara, narrowing her eyes at me. 'That's really sweet of you, Abby.'

'Can't you just tell her the truth?' asks Reece. 'That you and Tara are best friends forever, or whatever.'

'I did,' I say. 'More than once. And that's why she's started going crazy. She's been saying she's going to tell you what I said. She's basically been blackmailing me to be her friend.'

'What a freak,' Reece says.

Tara grimaces at me. 'I can't believe you told her she was your best friend.' She looks angry, but I know that's because she's really hurt. 'How could you?'

'There's more,' I tell her.

Tara swallows hard, preparing herself.

'She's got your friendship bracelet.'

Tara's mouth falls opens. 'What?! You said it was broken but you had it.'

'I know. I lied. And I feel really bad,' I say. 'I'm so sorry, Tara. But she took it from me and I've been trying to get it back from her, but you've seen how persistent she can be.'

Tara says nothing for a moment, she just looks thoughtful. Then, 'I would never do that to you,' she finally says, her jaw hardening. She crosses her arms.

'Just tell her to bug off,' says Reece.

'I've tried, but she's a real and actual psychopath!' I say, the full force of the situation hitting me. 'Look what she did tonight.'

'So how do you make her stop?' Reece asks.

'I've reported her on Facebook and Instagram.' I turn to Tara. 'But I think if *you* spoke to her and said you knew everything, she would have to stop, because she wouldn't have a hold over us any more.'

'You want me to call that cow?' says Tara. 'Your *best friend*.' She's sneering. I can't blame her.

'It's horrible, I know,' I say. 'But then it'll all be over.'

I hold out my hand for Reece's phone because Gerry won't pick up a call from me and there's more chance she might answer from a number she doesn't know. Reece gives me his phone. I tap Gerry's number in and press *Call*.

'Hello?' says Gerry. She's panting.

'Gerry,' I say. 'It's Abby.'

Reece and Tara come close so they can hear what Gerry's saying.

'Oh, *you*,' she says. 'Calling me from someone else's phone? Now you know what it's like to be ignored.'

'I never ignored you, Gerry,' I say. 'I just—'

'Who are you with?' asks Gerry.

'I'm with the person you've been harassing. Did you chase Tara in the park just now?'

'I don't know what you're talking about,' she says, but she sounds so smug.

'Liar,' hisses Tara.

'I'm at home,' she says.

'Now *that's* a lie,' I tell her. 'You just checked in in Wimbledon.'

Quick as a flash she says, 'My Facebook account's been hacked.'

There is no point in arguing – she'll have an answer for everything, I'm sure. 'Look, whatever,' I say. 'I'm calling you to tell you to leave Tara alone.'

'I don't—'

'Leave me alone too,' I say. 'I don't want to be friends with you any more. Delete my number, take me off your Instagram, defriend me on Facebook. Never contact me again.'

Gerry's gone quiet.

'I mean it. I want you out of my life. Forever.'

There's a pause. 'What if I don't want to?' says Gerry. 'It takes two people to stay away. And I don't think you want to piss me off right now. What if I tell Tara all the things she never knew about her best friend?'

'Tara knows,' I say. 'I told her everything.'

'I don't believe you,' Gerry scoffs.

'Here,' I say, 'speak to her. She's been listening the whole time.'

I pass the phone to Tara, who looks somewhere between nervous and angry.

'Gerry,' she says, 'it's Tara. I hate you for what you've done. Stay away from me from now on. And stay away from Abby too. I know she said you were her best friend, and she let you take my bracelet, but she didn't mean it, OK? Abby wouldn't do anything mean to me on purpose.' She takes a deep breath. 'Find your own friends.' Tara's voice is steady and calm, but I can tell she's seething underneath it. 'Stop being a psychopath and just let it go.'

I wince a little – that was harsh. But totally deserved. There's no way Gerry hasn't got the message now.

'What?' says Tara. Her tone has changed. Gerry's said something she's interested in. Tara turns away from me. 'What do you mean?'

I start feeling anxious. A minute ago Tara and I were united against Gerry, but now . . . Tara throws a look at me over her shoulder.

'No, she didn't,' she says. 'What did she write?'

I start feeling sick. I know what's happening. Gerry's telling her about the drawing.

Tara turns back to me, her teeth clenched. 'Did you take the mick out of me behind my back?'

Reece looks awkward. He can tell this is a big deal and Tara and I are about to have a *big* fight.

'I . . .' There's no room for lies any more. I nod.

Tara looks like I have just slapped her. 'Right,' she says to me. She looks down at the phone. 'So there, you see,' she says to Gerry. 'Now I do know everything. Leave us the hell alone.'

She stabs at the phone and hands it back to Reece. Then she falls forward into his arms and he hugs her. There's no one to hug me.

'I can't believe you,' she mumbles.

'I'm so, so sorry, Tara,' I say. 'I'll make it up to you.'

Tara's not looking at me. She has her head on Reece's shoulder, looking the other way.

'But at least it is definitely over now,' I say. 'There's no more secrets – Gerry can't blackmail me any more. It's done.'

Reece's phone beeps. Tara takes it from his hand and stares at it. She zooms in and scrolls around the screen.

She takes so long that I know just what it is. A photo of the drawing. Tara gasps and covers her hand with her mouth. 'You did all that?'

'I didn't . . .' But I'm not going to deny it.

'Gerry started it and I got carried away. I was a bit angry with you. I should've never—'

'You're right, Abby,' she says.

I hope she's going to forgive me, but her face is pale and she's angrier than I've ever seen her.

'You should've never betrayed me like that. It *is* all over. After everything you've done, I don't want to be your friend any more.'

'But—'

Tara pulls Reece's arm, and they walk away from me in the direction of his house. My heart sinks. These are words I never thought I would hear Tara say. We've had our ups and downs before but we've always got through them.

'But we're best friends forever,' I say feebly.

She stops and looks back at me. 'We *were* best friends,' she says. 'But nothing's forever. Now we're not even friends.'

And with that she walks away down the street, leaving me standing alone.

I've just lost the most important person in my entire life.

And it's all my own fault.

Chapter 24

I walk slowly back to my house. I don't care who sees me crying now. I try to think of ways I can make it up to Tara – buy her something, or write her a letter. Maybe if I told her exactly what happened while I was away it would all be different. But I should have told her when it happened, not left it till I was forced to.

It's Gerry's fault too though. I really think she might be crazy. She seemed so nice when I met her – wacky, yeah – but really fun. This isn't how normal people behave. Even when someone has been as stupid as I have. Why is she like this?

My phone beeps. I hope it's Tara, and if it *is* Tara, I hope she's telling me that we'll make up eventually, not telling me to pick up my stuff from her house.

It's Gerry. Maybe she's apologizing, or begging me to be her friend again. But whatever

she says, I'm never talking to her again. The
damage has been done.

I tap my phone to read the message.

This is not going to stop.

A threat. But what more could she do to me?
Tara doesn't want to be my friend any more.
Gerry's won. There's nothing left.

I'm angry now. I start typing back:

*What part of DELETE MY NUMBER do you not
understand? Leave me—*

But another text comes in before I've finished.
This time it's Becky.

*You are the best sister ever. I've been speaking to my
friends about you. We both agree that you are ace.
I love you x x*

At least Becky loves me. She's a great little sister
and I don't tell her enough. We never say we
love each other. We probably should . . .

Hang on.

That text doesn't sound like Becky at all. She never sends soppy messages – usually just jokes. Never *I love you*, or *you're ace*. In fact, I've never heard her use the word 'ace' in her entire life.

Oh God. Gerry's got her.

I run.

I'm still running as I rush through the front door. 'Mum!' I shout. If anything's happened to Becky I will never forgive myself. 'Becky!'

Mum emerges round the door of the TV room, but I am already halfway up the stairs. 'Abby,' she says, frowning deeply. 'What's the matter?'

'Where's Becky?' I ask her.

'Upstairs of course,' she says. 'What's wrong?'

'Is she OK?'

'She's fine. Why?'

I carry on running up the stairs to check for myself.

'What is wrong with you, Abigail?' my mum

calls after me. 'And why didn't you tell me your friend was coming round?'

Gerry's here. She could be doing something to Becky right now while Mum's oblivious downstairs. I had no idea Gerry was a psychopath, so how would Mum guess it?

I don't know what I'm expecting to see when I push the door to her room. Becky with a knife to her throat? Becky already dead? I'm hoping I've got here in time.

I smash into the door, then twist the handle.

'Becky!' I shout as I open it.

She's there. Smiling. She looks really happy.

'What's up, big sis?' she says.

I am so relieved I could cry. The Becky Lump is bigger than ever now because I never thought something *I* did would harm her. But I brought Gerry into our lives.

'Did you get my message?' Becky asks. 'We spent a lot of time coming up with it.'

We.

The door closes. Gerry is standing there, hiding behind the door.

'Surprise,' she says, smiling sweetly as if the

264

last half-hour never happened. 'Bet you never thought you'd see *me* in your house.' She widens her eyes.

'A big surprise,' I say quietly. 'What're you doing here?'

'How rude is *she*?' she asks Becky, thumbing at me.

Becky laughs.

I feel sick.

'I think you should leave now, Gerry,' I say to her, giving her a look that Becky can't see so she knows I'm serious.

'But she only just arrived,' says Becky, whining. She likes Gerry. She doesn't know any better.

'Becky wants me to stay,' says Gerry. 'I'm Becky's guest too, so you can't tell me to leave.'

Wow. Just when I think this girl can't sink any lower.

'I *can* tell you to leave,' I say to Gerry. 'Get the—'

'Abby!' Becky screeches. 'Why are you being so mean?'

'Yeah, Abby,' says Gerry, and she goes to

265

stand by Becky's bed. 'Stop being a big *fat* meanie.'

Becky giggles as she looks up at Gerry.

'Get out now,' I say, not bothering to hide it from Becky. 'Before I get my mum up here and tell her everything.'

I can make threats too. I have nothing left to lose. But somehow it's not getting through. Gerry's beaming like she has one last trick up her sleeve.

'Abby,' says Becky, and her smile is gone, 'please don't be mean to Gerry.' She pleads with her eyes. I wish I could make her understand, but she's too little. 'Gerry's doing something so massive. We can't *ever* be mean to her.'

What's she up to now? The Gerry Dread is lodged in my throat and it's choking me.

'Will you tell her or shall I?' Gerry whispers to Becky, just loud enough so I can hear.

Becky nods; she's going to be the one to deliver the news. 'Gerry went and got herself tested,' she says. Her eyes are shining she's so happy. 'She has the same blood type as me! Same tissue type too.'

My stomach starts to churn.

'She's a perfect match!'

I feel my mouth filling up with saliva.

'Gerry's going to give me her kidney!'

My legs go wobbly.

'Isn't this great?' says Becky. 'She'll be like my big sister and saviour rolled into one. We owe her everything!'

'I'll settle for being your friend,' Gerry says sweetly.

'Best friends,' says Becky.

I cover my mouth with my hand.

'We'll be best friends forever,' says Gerry, stroking Becky's hair. She looks at me. 'Isn't that great?'

Gerry has found the ultimate way to wheedle herself into my life. I can never get rid of her.

I run to the toilet and throw up.

Chapter 25

The bell goes for lunch and the girls get up and walk out. Tara won't sit next to me any more so I have to sit next to one of the boys – Kyle Rosen. He won't speak to me either, but I think that has more to do with me being a girl than anything I've done to Tara.

Donna throws me a nasty look as she puts her arm round Tara. 'Come on, Tara,' she says. 'Let's get lunch.'

Which is so hypocritical – Donna's always hated Tara. But I guess she just likes getting in the middle of all the drama, jumping on the Hate Abby bandwagon.

The girls aren't really my main problem at the moment. I miss Tara so much, but I'm more worried about Becky and what Gerry's planning to do to her. Mum doesn't seem to know about the kidney thing, so I might have some time.

But if Gerry's not lying, and she's willing to give up a body part to superglue herself into my life, then she's more messed up than I thought. Would Mum and Dad let Gerry do it? Could they refuse if Gerry insists? I wonder if I should even be thinking of refusing it. Maybe having a crazy person in my life is a price worth paying to get Becky well.

If only I could be sure she meant it.

'Obi!' I call to her as she files out of the classroom after the others.

Obi looks back at me. Then looks at the girls, who are already through the door, trying to decide what to do.

'What do *you* want?' she says, scowling.

'Talk to me for a minute,' I say to her. 'Please.'

She sighs, then comes over. 'OK,' she says. When she gets to me she looks me in the eye. 'What you did was really lame, Abby. You betrayed Tara, and let's face it – you weren't very nice to Gerry either.' She tilts her head. 'It's actually Gerry I feel sorry for.'

If only she knew the truth. 'You can't feel sorry for her,' I say. 'She's completely mad.'

Obi squints at me, doubtful. 'You're the one in the wrong here, Abby,' she says sternly.

'I know!' I say. 'I'm not trying to defend what I did, just listen . . .' And I tell her everything; all about how my sister got ill on holiday and Gerry was there. And how she was really sweet, said I was her best friend, so when she asked me if I was hers I didn't feel I could say no, which was dumb, but then she took my bracelet from my wrist. How I drew a nice picture of Tara which Gerry got me to deface. Then how she stalked me – hounded me online, persuaded me and my friends to like her, stole things, showed up at the hospital when I said I couldn't see her. How she tagged along on my date with Joel by saying her friend stole her boyfriend from her. Then started dating Joel. Then slashed my bike tyres and chased Tara.

'And now she's offering . . . threatening . . . offering to give Becky her kidney. That's not normal, is it?' I ask Obi.

'No!' she says, pulling a disgusted face. 'I don't think so. I mean, it's one thing being nice,

270

but to offer a kidney to a girl you met four weeks ago is pretty weird.'

'Exactly!' Finally someone is listening to me.

'Could you speak to her parents about it?'

'I don't know her parents. They came to the open day, but I never met them. I don't even know where she lives.'

'How much *do* you know about this girl?' she asks.

'Almost nothing. I've never been to her house, I don't know her address. I have her mobile number, obviously, but she won't answer the phone to me any more. All I have is her name.'

'Do you know what school she goes to?' asks Obi.

'Yes!' I say. Of course. 'Barnet High, somewhere up in north London.'

'Maybe they'd give you her address,' she suggests. But she shakes her head at exactly the same time as I do. There's no way they would give out a student's details, not even if I say I'm one of her friends.

'We have to go up there,' I say, 'and find her.'

Obi bites her lip. 'When?'

'Today,' I say. 'Now. We're going to have to bunk off.'

'We can't do that,' says Obi. 'I have Mr Raza this afternoon.'

'Please come with me, Obi,' I beg her. 'It's a matter of life and death.'

People say that phrase a lot, but this time it actually feels true. I have a horrible feeling that someone is going to really get hurt because of this – me, my sister, Tara . . . I don't know. I just know we have to stop Gerry before it's too late.

'All right, let's go,' says Obi. 'Where's this school then?'

Now it's my turn: Gerry, I'm coming to get you.

Chapter 26

It's just after 3 p.m. when we finally get to Barnet High school. It's taken us nearly two hours to get here. School hasn't finished yet, and there's no one outside the gates.

'We'll wait until she comes out,' I say. 'She should be easy enough to spot, with those red curls. Then when she does, we'll follow her home. Once she's in, we'll speak to her mum and dad, see if they can sort her out.'

Obi nods. 'They probably have no idea how crazy she is.'

I'm sure they don't. How could they?

We hear a bell ring inside the school and immediately kids start pouring out. It's just a few at first, but then more and more. And I can't spot Gerry anywhere.

'What if we miss her?' I say to Obi, beginning to panic.

Obi starts pulling at the hair on the back of her neck. 'What if she sees us before we see her?' It's rare for Obi to be nervous.

'Let's ask,' I say. I walk up to a nice-looking girl with an armful of books. 'Excuse me,' I say.

She looks at me, then at my uniform, confused. 'Yes?'

'Do you know someone called Gerry Barnes?'

The girl wrinkles her nose and her glasses fall down her face. 'Who?'

'Gerry – Geraldine – Barnes,' I say. 'She has auburn curly hair.'

'What class is she in?'

'I don't know,' I say, 'but she's in Year 8.'

The girl shrugs. 'I'm in Year 8,' she says, 'and I've never heard of Gerry Barnes.'

How can this girl not know someone in her own year? 'How big is this school?'

'I know everyone in Year 8, if that's what you mean. There's no Gerry Barnes.'

My head starts spinning. I don't understand.

From the look on Obi's face, she doesn't understand either. 'Are you sure we got the right school?' she asks me.

An obvious question pops into my head. 'Do we even have the right name?' I say aloud. If not, Gerry would have been using a fake name from the very beginning, which makes her so much more sinister. But from everything I know now, I wouldn't put it past her.

'Do you have a photo?' the girl asks.

Genius! I get out my phone. The first place I think of is Facebook, but then I remember that I defriended her. In a way, I wish I hadn't. It means I have no idea where she is or what she's up to.

I start scrolling through my photos for photos of us together. I have a few . . . but you can't see Gerry properly in any of them. There are loads of me that she's taken, but none of her. I get to a selfie of us both, but her head is turned to the side so you can only see a quarter of her face. The next is of her, but she's pulled a hat over her eyes.

Obi's looking at the photos over my shoulder. 'Do you think she hides in photos on purpose?'

I don't know any more. Gerry could have been planning this since the moment she met me.

'Look, I have to go,' says the girl, and she starts walking away.

But I can't give up. There must be some way to find her.

'Ellie Poole!' I say. The girl who stole Gerry's boyfriend.

The girl stops and turns to us again, this time with more recognition on her face.

'Do you know Ellie Poole?' I ask. 'Or a boy called Mack?'

The girl smiles now. 'Yeah,' she says. 'She's just over there.' She's pointing to a group of girls standing by a tree in front of the school. 'The girl with the hat and blue bag. That's Ellie.'

'Thank you so much,' I say, and Obi and I run over to them.

The girls hear us approach and turn to stare at us.

'Er . . . hi,' I say to the girl with the blue bag. 'Are you Ellie Poole?'

The girl nods and looks understandably suspicious. 'What do you want?'

Her friends edge closer to her. I like the way

they stand up for each other; I'd do the same for my friends.

'Do you know someone called Gerry Barnes?'

Ellie frowns in the same way the girl frowned before – I can tell straight away that she's never heard the name before. It doesn't surprise me; I'm convinced now that this isn't her real name.

'She has curly auburn hair, about this long?' I put my hand up to my shoulder. 'Pretty, but a bit . . . wild.'

Ellie's face drains of colour. 'Who are you?'

One of her friends puts an arm around her. 'Did she send you?' the friend asks, looking angry. 'I'll call the teacher.' She looks back towards the school. There are some teachers in the car park.

'Please,' says Obi. 'We're not here to cause trouble, we just want to know where she lives.'

'Why?' Ellie's friend says.

I recognize this reaction, I recognize it from the way I feel – it's the Gerry Dread. Ellie Poole has gone through something similar.

'I don't know you, Ellie,' I say to her gently,

'but I think we both know the same person, and she's a bit of a psychopath.'

'A bit!' spits her friend. 'That's an understatement!'

'I met a girl when I was away at half-term,' I explain. 'She said her name was Gerry, but I think she was lying.'

Ellie's paying close attention now.

'She told me about you . . . but now, I think she was lying about that too.'

Ellie gets her phone from her handbag and scrolls through her photos. 'Is this her?' she shows me a photo of Ellie and 'Gerry' with their arms around each other.

I nod.

'That's from when we used to be friends,' she says. 'We're not any more.'

'What happened?' asks Obi.

Ellie hesitates.

'She told me that you stole her boyfriend,' I offer.

The girls standing around her all gasp at the same time.

'I'm guessing that's not what happened.'

Ellie gulps. 'No,' she says, 'it's not what happened.'

'Are you OK, Ellie?' her friend asks. 'You don't have to talk to them if you don't want to.'

Whatever happened to Ellie, it must have been serious for them all to be so protective.

'I just want to know the truth, before she does something terrible to the people I love.'

Ellie nods and I can tell she's being brave. She takes a deep breath and begins. 'Her name is Sophie Ross – I don't know where she got Gerry Barnes from.'

Sophie Ross – her first lie. She told it the very first moment we met.

'We were once really good friends – *best* friends really. We used to hang out all the time. We've been close since primary school.'

An image of Tara flashes in my mind.

'At the end of September, I started going out with a boy.'

'Mack?' I ask.

She nods.

'Gerry – Sophie – said he was *her* boyfriend,' I tell her.

Ellie's friend raises her eyebrows at her friends. 'Why doesn't that surprise me?' she mutters.

'I tried not to leave Sophie out, but of course I wanted to spend time alone, just me and Mack. Sophie kept getting jealous.'

Again, I think of Tara and how jealous I got when she obsessed over Reece.

'Did she never expect me to get a boyfriend, ever?' says Ellie.

It's mates over boys . . . but you have to have a little room for boyfriends.

'One time, my phone went missing from my bag.' She puts her hand on her bag now, as if checking it's still closed. 'I tried to message Mack from my laptop to let him know I'd lost it, but he wouldn't reply to my messages. Turns out, she's the one who stole it. She'd been messaging Mack from my phone, pretending to be me, telling him I didn't like him any more.'

That sounds like the Gerry I know.

'She dumped him.'

Now it's Obi's turn to gasp. 'Conniving cow!'

'Then she arranged to meet him,' Ellie says. 'She told me she was doing it for me, that she was going to help me to get back together with him. But when they met up, she jumped on him and tried to kiss him. He pushed her away. Then he told me about it.'

This sounds like what she did with me and Joel.

'When I confronted her . . .' Ellie's voice is shaky, 'she attacked me.'

'That's awful,' says Obi.

'Attacked you how?' I ask. 'Physically?'

Ellie's friend nods. 'We had to call the police.'

I have to stop this before the same thing happens to me. I'm terrified of seeing Gerry again, but I have to tell her to back off. Speaking to her parents is the only way.

'Do you have any idea where she is now?' I ask.

Ellie shakes her head. 'Luckily, she's stayed away. I haven't seen her in ages,' she says. 'She was expelled the week before half-term.'

Just before I met her.

'I wouldn't go after her, if I were you,' Ellie's friend says. 'She can be dangerous.'

'I have to,' I say. My sister could be in danger if I don't stop Gerry.

The friend nods at Ellie. 'Show them,' she says.

Ellie sighs and takes off her hat. Underneath, her hair is only an inch long.

Obi covers her mouth in shock.

'Did Gerry – Sophie – do that to you?' I ask.

Ellie nods. 'This is after the hairdresser did her best to tidy it up. Sophie held me down and cut chunks of my hair off. It was only when Mack came in that she put down the scissors. Otherwise, I don't know what she would have done.'

So Gerry is violent as well as crazy. But I can't back off now. I have to stop her before she does something really bad to someone I love.

Chapter 27

Gerry (or Sophie, or whoever she really is) lives down a set of streets that seem like a series of dark alleyways with mostly broken street lamps. It's outside of Barnet — another bus ride away. Ellie warned Obi and me that if we planned to go to her house we should do it before it got too late — apparently the area isn't a good place to be at night time. It *is* late. And dark. The police told us not to come, that they would deal with it. But I need to make sure for myself that it's all over.

Gerry told me she was rich and lived in a nice street where every house had a massive garden. She even told me one of her neighbours had an indoor pool. Yet more lies.

I'm clutching the piece of paper where Ellie wrote Gerry's address. It's along this street somewhere — number 133. We're at number 119. Not far. I hope the police come soon.

We reach number 133. It doesn't look too bad, but the bushes in the front garden are overgrown and there's a can full of cigarette butts by the door.

Obi looks at me. 'Ready?' she asks. I nod, and she knocks.

There's shuffling from inside. Then lots of clicking noises as someone unlocks various locks on the front door.

Obi and I look at each other and take a deep breath. She's just as scared as I am, and that doesn't feel good.

The door opens just a crack. We only get a glimpse of the woman's face behind it. She's scowling at us. 'Yes?'

'Ms Ross?' I say. 'I'm Sophie's friend. Can we come in, please?'

'She's not in,' she says through the gap.

Good. This might be easier without her here.

'Actually it's you and Mr Ross we'd like to talk to,' says Obi.

The woman sighs. 'There isn't a Mr Ross,' she says.

Gerry told me her dad was around – she

spoke about him all the time. Obviously another lie.

Finally the door opens fully and the woman lets us in. She closes the door behind us and the first thing that hits me is the smell of cigarette smoke. Ms Ross has red hair pulled back tight in a bun. She's short – even shorter than me – and she looks exhausted.

This is not the woman Gerry pointed out when she came to visit the school. But I have seen this woman before.

I ran out of the post office looking for Gerry.

Where had she got to? 'Gerry!' I hissed. But there was no reply. 'Gerry!' I shouted louder.

Then I remembered the stolen Aero in my pocket. I should have turned back and paid for it. But I was too scared. Gerry had run off and I knew she was up to something. I'd known the girl for less than a week and worked out by now that her *wild side* was a bit more than that. How could I have let myself be sucked in?

Outside the village post office was a single-track road lined with hedges. Gerry stuck her head round one of the hedges and waved me over.

'Where did you run off to?' I asked her. 'That lady was nice and . . .'

But I trailed off when I saw what Gerry was pulling out of her pockets: a pencil. A pack of cute rubbers. She opened her jacket and took out a stack of A4 envelopes. Then a cheesy, plastic bucket and spade.

My face fell. 'Where did you get them from?' I asked. But I knew.

Gerry's eyes twinkled as she wiggled her eyebrows.

'Did you pay for that?' I asked.

She guffawed.

'But . . . You shoplifted!'

Gerry shrugged. 'Yeah. So?' The dark look was back and I didn't like it.

This is not how I'd thought my nice family holiday would turn out. But me and my aunt and uncle were going home the next day. If I was honest, I would be glad to get a break from Gerry. It had all been pretty intense.

'I don't know, Gerry,' I said. 'I think we should give it back. You'll get in trouble.'

'What about you?' said Gerry, her voice gravelly. 'You stole too.'

My fingers closed around the chocolate bar in my pocket. I *had* stolen. Who was I becoming? I didn't want to be Boring Flabby Abby any more, but I definitely didn't want to become *this* person.

'I'm returning this,' I said firmly. 'And I'm taking your stuff too.' I grabbed the envelopes from her.

'Hey!' she said, her eyes flashing furiously.

I turned away and went round the hedge back on to the pavement. And bumped straight into a woman. She had red hair, pulled back in a bun and she was very short.

She looked me up and down, and smiled when she caught sight of the things I had piled in my arms. She must have heard me and Gerry behind the hedge, saying how we stole all this stuff. My heart sank. We were in big trouble now.

'Five-fingered discount, eh?' the woman said with a smirk.

'Huh?' I said, my face burning.

'Did you nick them, or what?' she asked.

'I . . . er . . . No.' My face burned. I was terrified she might tell the nice old lady in the shop and she'd call the police. My parents had enough to worry about with my sister in hospital. The last thing they needed was a daughter who was a criminal.

But the way the woman smiled made me think she was OK with it. 'Don't worry, love.' She tapped her nose. I didn't think I'd ever met an adult like that before – one who actually approved of stealing.

Gerry appeared round the hedge.

'Oh,' said the woman, her face brightening at the sight of Gerry. 'Hello.'

Gerry didn't say anything, just pushed past her, glaring. She grabbed my hand and pulled me along with her. I allowed it. I was happy to get away.

'Picking yourself up some stuff?' the woman said as we walked off. 'Attagirl.'

Gerry stomped up the road, still dragging me with her.

'Who was that?' I asked.

Gerry glanced back at the woman for just a moment. 'Probably some chav from the caravan site.' Then she strode on.

I frowned. I didn't like the word *chav*. I knew all about being insulted because of the way I looked – people used to call me 'Flabby Abby' all the time. 'That's not nice, Gerry,' I said to her. 'You don't know anything about her.'

'I know enough.'

I was about to tell her what I thought of that when Gerry turned back to me. The dark look had vanished. 'Come on,' she said. 'I'm giving up my life of crime.' She smiled at me. It made me feel better, but not a lot. 'Let's go to your house and play cards.'

I'd be glad when tomorrow came and I could go home. The holiday had been a weird mixture of fun and stress. I wanted to get back to my real life and forget about it. I'd never mention any of this to anyone. Not the Boys' School Girls. Not Becky or my mum and dad. Not even Tara.

In fact, I planned to sneak off tomorrow and not even say goodbye. New Abby was finished, and so was my friendship with Gerry.

Somewhere behind us I heard the woman shout, 'Sophie!'

I figured she was calling someone else.

Now I know that woman is Gerry's mum. And Gerry called her a chav. How could she say that about her own mother?

She stares at us. 'Like I said, Sophie's not home.'

Just then, there's the sound of a key in the door behind us.

'Mum! How many times have I told you to double-lock . . . oh.'

'Sophie,' says her mum, 'your friends have come over.'

Sophie looks at me and Obi. 'What are you doing here?' she says.

But I think she knows.

Chapter 28

Gerry gulps a little when she sees me. She must know how much I know – the fake name, lying about her parents. I wonder if she realizes I recognize her mum from that day on holiday.

'Abby . . . Obi . . .' she says, forcing a smile. 'What's going on?'

'Umm . . .' I'm not really sure how to answer. I don't like getting people in trouble, but I do want her craziness to stop. 'Ger—' I correct myself. 'Sophie,' I say, and she winces. 'We need to talk.'

She frowns. 'Shouldn't you be at school?'

Obi gives a big huff beside me. Gerry's trying to deflect, pointing out that we're not so perfect for bunking school when she's been the one who has been acting . . . what? Bizarrely? Criminally? By chasing after Tara, did she actually break any laws?

'I want to talk to you – and your mum – about some of the stuff you've been doing,' I tell her, sounding a million times braver than I feel. 'It has to stop.'

Gerry's mum sighs like this isn't the first time she's had to have this kind of chat. 'Let's go into the sitting room.'

There isn't much furniture in the little house. Just a two-seater sofa, where me and Obi sit, and a circular dining table where her mum sits on one of the mismatched chairs.

Gerry drops her bag, and only now do I realize that, of course, she's not wearing school uniform. It's starting to make sense now – how she could be down to see me all the time when she lives miles away. How she came to the open day when it was on a school day. She's been expelled and hasn't been at school for weeks. Which means she was lying when I spoke to her and Mack and she said she was at school. Mack probably wasn't even there at all. I guess she pretended to be him.

She sits next to her mum, but there's no eye contact between them. They're really far away from each other, and her mum looks as if this is an issue with a naughty dog.

'I should tell you,' I say, 'that the police are coming.'

'What?!' Gerry yells, as if I'm being unfair.

Her mum shakes her head and rolls her eyes. 'Great,' she says. 'Now this will get back to Gerry.' She looks at me. 'Her social worker.'

It doesn't take a genius to work it out. 'Gerry Barnes?' I ask.

'Something like that,' says Ms Ross. She lights a cigarette.

I look up at Gerry but she won't look at me. Obi and I exchange a glance. If Obi ever doubted how weird Gerry was, now she knows the truth. In a way, I feel better — I haven't been imagining all this.

'Gerry,' I say, leaning forward on the sofa. 'Sophie. Why didn't you tell me your real name?'

She shrugs.

Her mum looks at me so I explain. I hope hearing it out loud will make Gerry realize how oddly she's been behaving. 'We met on holiday at half-term.'

Ms Ross smiles at the memory of the holiday.

'Your daughter was really nice to me and we became good friends. She wanted to be my best friend . . . but I already had one.' I look at Gerry now. 'I'm really sorry, but Tara has always been my best friend. I just said that you were because I didn't want to hurt your feelings And because . . . I didn't think I'd ever see you again.'

Gerry's got tears in her eyes. 'So you didn't really like me at all!'

'I did!' I say. 'But Tara and I have been best friends since we started primary school. Nothing is going to change that.'

'Who's this Tara girl?' her mum asks. 'Why isn't she here instead of –' she points at Obi – 'what's your name again?'

'Obi,' she tells her. 'I'm here because Tara isn't speaking to Abby at the moment. Kind of because of this.'

'Gerry . . . er, Sophie posted really nasty things about Tara online,' I tell her mum. 'She told Tara's boyfriend she was cheating on him . . . which she wasn't,' I add, in case that wasn't clear.

'I told you,' says Gerry, 'my account was hacked.'

'It's not like it was just spam,' says Obi, glaring at Gerry. 'You were attacking Tara specifically.'

'And you stole the boy I like – Joel. You made up some lie about Ellie Poole stealing your boyfriend, so I had to cancel my date with him.'

At the name *'Ellie Poole'* Gerry's mum takes interest, tutting and shaking her head.

'Then *you* went on a date with Joel.' My voice catches in my throat, and I have to take a deep breath to stop myself from bursting into tears. 'You knew how much I liked him.'

'He asked *me* out,' Gerry says.

'You chased Tara last night,' I say to her, but I'm looking at her mum. 'Tara was terrified.'

Ms Ross looks at her daughter now.

'I didn't!' she says. 'I was nowhere near there. I was with Becky – Abby's sister.'

She has an answer for everything. But it doesn't add up. 'You used Becky to get to me.'

'No . . . Becky invited me over.' Gerry folds her arms in front of her chest. She looks like a five-year-old in a sulk.

'Becky's too ill to have friends over,' I say. 'She knows that.' The Becky Lump mixes with the Gerry Dread and I can't hold it in any more. I start to cry. Obi puts her arm around me.

'After all I've done for you, you're calling the police on me!' Gerry says. 'It might make me take back my generous offer.' She looks at me and there's a threat in her voice. If I don't let this go, she won't give my sister her kidney.

But I've wised up to Gerry now.

'What's Sophie's blood type?' I ask her mum.

Gerry's head snaps up. She knows I have her here. 'No—' she starts to say, but her mum interrupts.

'What? I'm not sure,' says her mum. 'Group A, I think.'

Becky's is type B. This makes me really angry. She told my sister she would give her a kidney when there was absolutely no way she could. Becky thought she could get a new life,

296

but it was a lie. The biggest lie you could tell. 'How could you?' I growl at her.

Gerry has the sense not to say anything.

There's a knock at the door and her mum gets up to answer it. 'Ms Ross, it's the police,' says a female voice through the door.

I stand up and walk slowly towards Gerry, pointing my finger in her face. 'I will never ever forgive you for this.'

Two female police officers enter the room and look concerned about me threatening Gerry. Obi's there already and pulls me back.

'Becky has been through enough without you lying to her, getting her hopes up!' I yell, tears streaming down my face.

'What's all this about?' asks one of the officers, a slim woman with brown hair in a low ponytail. 'Are you the girls who called us? We told you to go home. We can deal with this.'

But I'm not budging. I have to tell them what she's done. 'My sister's seven years old,' I tell the police woman. 'She needs a kidney transplant.' I take a deep breath, pushing away the image of my little sister looking so happy at the thought of getting better. '*Sophie* told her she was a match. That she could give her one of her kidneys.'

Everyone looks outraged. Except for Gerry, who brings her hands up to her face and starts to weep.

'She said she'd had the tests and everything.'

Gerry's mum covers her mouth like she's going to be sick. 'You disgusting child! You have done some terrible things in your life, but this . . .' She waves her hands in the air. 'You can forget about your birthday next week. I'm cancelling it.'

Another bell goes off in my head. Her birthday is next week? That means it can't have been during half-term. I wonder if a single thing Gerry said to me was true.

'OK, girls,' the larger police officer says to me and Obi, 'it's time for you two to leave now.'

Obi's right beside me. We move towards the front door and I'm too shocked to speak.

'Abby!' Gerry shouts from the living room. 'Wait.'

Obi looks at me and I nod at her. I want to hear what Gerry has to say, so I walk back into the living room. There's nothing more Gerry can do to me now.

'Abby,' says Gerry, 'I'm so sorry.' Tears are pouring down her face. 'I was just a little . . . desperate. Ellie had left me and then I met you – and you were so nice and you said you'd be my best friend. I guess I sensed that we weren't *really* best friends, and that just made me want to hold on to you even tighter. That's why I sent you all those messages and acted all weird when we met up. I wanted to show your friends how fun I was so that they'd understand why you'd picked me. I wanted to be cool enough for you so you'd be my best friend. And when Becky needed a kidney . . . I wanted to give it to her. I honestly did.'

'And all that stuff you did to Tara?' I say, not even close to forgiving her.

'Just . . . Just tell Tara I'm really sorry. It won't happen again. I'll be starting a new school in the new year. I'll find new friends. It's over now. I'm going to stop.'

This is all I wanted to hear. Gerry's clearly a messed-up girl who has been through a lot. I want to forgive her. I don't know much about her life, but if she had to lie about it, then I know it can't be good. I should be more sympathetic.

'Please forgive me,' she adds.

I'll never be able to forget what she's done, but I don't want revenge either.

I clench my teeth together. 'I don't think so,' I say. 'But if Tara can forgive me for what I did to her – and if all the damage you caused gets cleared up – then maybe . . . in time.'

Beside me, Obi shudders.

'But we'll never be friends,' I tell her.

The sides of Gerry's mouth start to wobble. 'But . . .'

'Sorry,' I add.

Because I *am* sorry. As Obi and I walk out of the door and close it, I'm aware that behind us, Gerry's going to have to deal with all of this stuff. Her mum, the police, her social worker. Next term she'll be starting a new school – I only started Hillcrest a few months ago so I know how hard that is. Gerry has brought all this on herself, but that doesn't mean she wanted it to happen.

'It's all going to be fine now, Abs,' says Obi as we walk down the street to the bus stop.

And she's right. Now that Gerry's out of my life it's going to be fine. I just need to get everything back to the way it was.

Chapter 29

Dad pushes Becky in her wheelchair as we all head up the hill. Wimbledon Village looks amazing.

'Wow!' Becky says. 'It's so cool.'

They've strung Christmas lights across the high street, and blocked off traffic so everyone is walking in the road. There are loads of stalls selling food and gifts. I can see Mrs Martin at the Hillcrest High stall, she's handing out leaflets and talking up the school. All the shops are staying open until late, and lots of people have dressed up, so I don't feel so silly in my elf outfit. Becky's got a matching one which I made her.

It's me and my whole family. I can't remember the last time we were all out together.

'What would you like, darling?' Mum says to Becky.

'A toffee apple!' says Becky, excited.

'Not a toffee apple, sorry, honey. Too much sugar won't be good with your medication. How about some roasted chestnuts?'

Becky sticks her tongue out, making me laugh.

'I feel the same way about granola bars,' I half-whisper. 'They pretend to be a treat, but everyone knows they are – *bleurgh!* – healthy.' I shudder.

The pom-pom on Becky's elf hat wobbles when she laughs.

I haven't felt this good in ages. Becky is doing well, and I haven't heard from Gerry all week. I guess she's sticking to her word and she really is going to leave me alone. I told Becky the doctors made a mistake about Gerry's blood type. She took it really well – I knew she would; she's always been so strong. She said she didn't want another operation right now anyway, and something would happen when the time was right.

So it's finally over. I just wish I hadn't lost Tara because of it. She still won't talk to me.

'Boo!'

A couple of werewolves jump out in front of us.

Mum clutches her heart in an over-the-top way. Dad puts up his hands like he's some kind of ninja about to do kung fu. Becky laughs again. I whack the werewolf with my elf candy cane.

'Joel!' I say. 'You nearly gave my mum a heart attack. She's afraid of mice,' I tease him.

'*Mice?!*' says Joel. 'We're terrifying werewolves!'

I smirk so he knows I know that. 'But what have werewolves got to do with Christmas?'

Joel and the other werewolf – I assume it's Reece – look at each other. 'Er . . .' says Reece. 'We had these costumes from Halloween.'

Mum and Dad laugh.

I shake my head. This is typical of Joel – and one reason why I like him so much. 'Mum, Dad, this weremouse is my friend Joel from school. And you know Reece, Tara's boyfriend.'

'Is that Becky?' Reece says. 'You look great! I didn't recognize you.'

'Are you sure?' Becky says, raising her eyebrow. 'The wheelchair didn't kind of give it away?'

Reece doesn't know how to respond to that so we all laugh at him.

'You missed the celebrity guest turning on the Christmas lights,' Joel says to me.

'Oh no!' I say. 'Who was it?'

'Boris Becker,' says Joel, nodding in appreciation.

'Who?' says Becky.

'He used to be a tennis player,' says Dad.

Becky shrugs. She's not into sports personalities. 'Maybe next year it will be a boy band. Or even Sucker Punch!'

Joel grins. 'That would be awesome!'

I'm glad that Joel's getting on with my family, but I need to sort something out before I can be really happy.

'Have you seen any of the others?' I ask. 'Obi? Maxie or . . . um . . . Tara?' It's so weird that I can't say my best friend's name without stuttering.

'Not yet,' says Reece, 'but Tara said they'd

all be hanging out around the other end of the high street, as far away from the teachers at the Hillcrest stall as possible. We're off to meet them. Lenny's already there with Donna.'

They're all meeting up without me. Now I'm experiencing symptoms of FOMO – a dark sinking feeling in my stomach, a million thoughts about conversations I haven't been included in surging through my head so fast they make my brain hurt.

It must show on my face because Mum looks at me and says, 'Why don't you go along too? We can all meet up later. We'll be leaving shortly after the fireworks – just make sure you're back with us by then.'

'Are you sure?' I ask. Today was supposed to be a family outing, a celebration of Becky feeling better. 'You don't mind, Bex? Wait! In fact, you can come too if you like.'

'Puh-lease,' she says, waving her hand at me. 'You'd cramp my style.' She's joking, but I can tell she's a bit sad. She doesn't go to school enough to have the kind of friends I do.

'Well, as long as you're sure.' I give Mum a serious look to check she's really OK with it. 'I'll meet you back here in an hour,' I say. 'Or call me.'

Mum nods. 'Go have fun.'

Reece, Joel and I walk along the high street. It's a bit weird being around both of them – last time I saw Reece out of school, me and his girlfriend were having a huge fight. And then there's the Joel-and-Gerry thing. I don't even know if they're together. Maybe they're still a couple and he speaks to her all the time. I have to think of a way to subtly ask him about it, then warn him off in a way that doesn't come across as jealousy.

'So . . . um . . . have you seen that new alien-attack movie yet?' I say, knowing it's the film he went to see with her.

Joel scrunches up his face. 'Yeah – what was the deal with you that night?'

'Huh?'

'Gerry and I waited ages but you never showed up . . . and you didn't answer her calls. We had to go in and watch it without you.'

'Whaaaa . . . ?' I ask, not able to create actual words as I try to make sense of what he just said. But then it starts to sink in – it's all another one of Gerry's lies. I'm beginning to lose count. 'What day was this again?'

'The other week,' he says, rubbing his scruffy hair. 'Gerry said you were both meeting up and going to the Imax, but when I got there you hadn't shown.'

He sounds genuinely upset, and my heart could float out of my mouth I'm so happy. He wanted me there. He only went on a '*date*' with Gerry because she said I'd be there.

'Sorry about that,' I say, trying to hide my smile. 'How was it?'

'The film was OK,' he says, 'I think.'

'You *think*?'

He rolls his eyes. 'Gerry didn't stop talking the whole time.'

I am tempted to tell Joel the truth about Gerry, but it seems he's found it out on his own. Besides, Gerry's gone now – she's out of our lives – for good.

'Well, I haven't seen it,' I tell him, trying

my best to sound totally calm about the whole thing. 'If you, you know, want to see it again.'

'Yeah,' says Joel. 'That'd be good.' And even in the darkness I can tell he's blushing. I have basically asked him out and he has basically said yes and I was really cool about it. I couldn't be more proud of myself if I tried. Maybe some of New Abby is still around after all. Go me!

'Hey,' says Reece, 'I want to see it too. Can we come?'

'We?' I ask.

'Me and Tara,' he says. 'We could make it a double date.'

Calling it a date has just ruined the coolness I set up and it's making me blush too. Normally I would want Tara there to help me out, to make me look OK in front of Joel. But Tara doesn't like me any more. 'Tara wouldn't want to go with me,' I say.

'Course she would,' says Reece, with a frustrated sigh like he's bored of the both of us.

'She hates me.' *And I don't blame her,* I add to myself.

'She misses you,' Reece tells me.

'No, she doesn't.' I sound like Donna when she's in a sulk.

'She won't stop going on about it!' Now he's the one complaining. 'I keep telling her that if she misses you so much she should just call you and make up. She says she wants to but your fight felt so final.' Reece shakes his head. 'I don't get girls. If Joel and I had a punch-up, after a few days we'd be back playing football, no problem. You lot have to talk about everything and analyse everything that was said for a million years before you make up.'

Joel does a fake shudder, making his werewolf fur shake. 'I don't get it either, mate,' he says.

I can't quite believe what I'm hearing. 'So . . . Tara wants to be friends again?'

'Of course she does!' says Reece, throwing his hands in the air. 'Just speak to her, will you? I'm sick of her going on about you all the time.'

'Now you know how *I* feel when she's going on about *you*,' I say.

This is the best news ever. Even better than the fact Joel didn't mean to go on a date with Gerry, *and* would actually like to go on a date with me. Tara means more to me than anything.

'Where is she?' I ask him, suddenly desperate to make this right, and to do it *right now*. I have to talk to her and see if she'll be my best friend again.

Reece glances at his phone as if the answer is there. 'At the end of the high street near the common. By the bookshop.'

I start running, my red and white striped tights a blur as I go. There are so many people out tonight that I have to pull up my mask so I can see my way through. The smells of mulled wine and roast chestnuts fill my nose.

I get halfway down the high street when I hear someone calling me.

'Abby! Abs!' they shout. 'We're over here.'

I turn and see a group of people dressed in greens and reds, all with hats and elf masks – it's the girls. And Tara must be with them.

I go over and when I get nearer it's easy to identify who's who. Donna's bought her mask from somewhere. It has a cute pixie look to it and her hair is flowing out round the sides. Sonia's tried to do the same, but her mask is home-made and it hasn't worked as well. Indiana has peace symbols all over her mask, which doesn't really go with the elf theme. Hannah's mask somehow looks moody, but pretty good really. Candy's curly hair is popping out the end of her green hat, it looks like it's about to fly off. And Obi's glittery mask looks really awesome against her dark skin. Maxie's done hers all geometrically – I think Tara said she YouTubed something about how to make the perfect one. It looks great – she's not a genius for nothing. Lenny's here too, but he's not dressed up. He looks really funny surrounded by all these elves, like he's lost in Lapland.

Tara isn't here.

'I love what you've done with the diamonds,' says Obi, pointing to my mask.

'Where's Tara?' I ask. 'I need to speak to her.'

Maxie gives a huff. She clearly hasn't forgiven me for what I did. That's OK – I haven't forgiven myself.

'Please, Maxie,' I say, 'do you know where she is? I really, really want to make up.'

Maxie sighs. 'She went off to find you.'

'That's great!' I say. 'Do you know which way she went?'

'That way.' She points. 'Towards the common. Isn't that where you're meeting her?'

That's where Reece said she would be. He must have messaged her to say I was coming.

'OK, thanks,' I say. 'I'll go find her and we'll see you back here in a bit.'

I race off again, so glad that I'm not as unfit as I used to be.

'She might be with Gerry,' says Hannah.

This stops me in my tracks. 'What?'

'I saw Gerry earlier,' says Hannah.

Everyone turns to Hannah.

'What's Gerry doing here?' asks Obi. She looks at me, as worried as I am.

'You saw Gerry?' says Maxie. She looks worried too. She must know about what happened with Gerry from Tara. 'When?'

'Why would she be with Tara?' asks Candy. 'Wasn't she a complete bitch to her on Facebook?'

'This is not good,' I say, almost to myself. 'We have to find her.'

'Who?' asks Indiana. 'Tara or Gerry?'

'Both . . . either. I'm worried Gerry might do something.'

Seven masked faces look at me anxiously. I get out my phone and text Gerry.

I thought you were going to stay away.

I wait for a reply. I don't know if I want one or not.

'Are you sure it was Gerry you saw, Hannah?' I ask. My heart is racing.

'Yeah,' says Hannah, looking really nervous as if she's done the wrong thing by even seeing her. 'I spoke to her. She was in a hurry. She said she was going to get Tara and then get you. Then she ran off.'

Oh God. Gerry's going to *get* us. Her screw must have come loose again. I suppose there's a chance she's come down here to apologize. But even that's not good – I just want her gone.

My phone beeps. The Gerry Dread returns.
A text back.

It's not over.

Oh God. I have to find Tara. Now.

Chapter 30

I hold the phone in my hand. This message is a direct threat. Gerry's out to get me, and Hannah said she's going to get Tara first. My head feels strangely light.

'Girls,' I say, hoping they understand how serious this is, 'I need your help. Gerry's a psychopath and I think she's going to hurt Tara.'

'Really?' asks Candy.

'No way,' says Hannah.

'Why would she hurt Tara?' asks Donna.

'It's true,' says Obi, backing me up. 'Gerry's real name is Sophie. And she's not normal.'

Donna raises an eyebrow, not quite believing her.

'The police are involved,' Obi adds.

The girls want more of an explanation but there's no time. 'We need to split up and look for them,' I say. 'Please help me.' I'm starting to feel panicky now. If Gerry could cut her best friend's hair off, what would she do to someone whose guts she really hates? Maybe Ellie Poole was just practice and now she's moving on to something worse. 'Call as soon as you see either of them.'

'What's your new number?' asks Maxie, her face the palest of everyone's.

'What? I don't have a . . .' But it all starts to make sense.

'Tara said you messaged her from a new phone,' she finishes.

So Reece didn't message Tara. And neither did I. It was Gerry, pretending to be me.

Just then there is a whizzing noise, then a huge bang and the street lights up for a second. The fireworks display has started. People move towards the end of the street where the display is. I'm heading in the opposite direction.

I start running. 'Same old number!' I shout back to them. 'Hurry!'

I don't think I've ever run so fast in all my life. I imagine a million scenarios, from the good – where Tara's waiting for me, completely unaware that anything's up – to the bizarre –

Tara and Gerry have made up and they are holding hands and sharing a toffee apple – to the really, really bad – Tara face down in a puddle with Gerry pushing her head.

Another bang fills the air. People around me ooh and ahh.

I have to find her. I realize now that this isn't my fault. Yes, I didn't handle things very well, but this has gone beyond madness. Gerry is actually insane and I'm terrified about what she's going to do to my friend.

'Tara!' I shout. 'Tara!' People are looking at me. They can tell I'm panicking.

'Tara!' I hear a voice right behind me. I turn, and I'm so glad to see Obi's here too.

'Tara!' we both call again.

We're slowed by a bunch of people on their way to see the fireworks.

'Excuse me. Excuse me,' I say as I elbow my way through.

'Are you girls all right?' a woman asks us. She's a middle-aged lady wearing a Santa hat.

I'm torn between answering her and moving on. Which will find Tara more quickly? More explosions light the street in weird, unnatural flashes.

'We've lost our friend,' Obi says, panting.

'What does she look like?' the lady asks.

'She wearing a mask like ours,' I say.

The woman's face brightens. 'I did see a girl dressed like you . . . But don't worry – she's not on her own. There was one, then another right after her. They were heading that way.' She points towards the common.

I don't even say thank you. Fortunately the crowds thin at this end so I can go even faster. Obi's still running along next to me, but we've both stopped calling out now. We can see more – there's a stall selling Christmas trees and wreaths . . . but no girls dressed as elves.

We get to the end of the high street, where it hits the common. There's no one around now. It's dark. I'm scared.

'Arggggh!' Obi roars in frustration. 'Where is she?'

I'm too frantic to answer. Did we pass her? I look around desperately. 'Tara . . . !' I yell as loud as I can.

It might be my imagination, but I think I hear someone cackle like a witch. This is a nightmare.

A succession of bangs go off, making my ears ring.

'Call Reece,' I say to Obi. 'See if she's with him.'

Obi gets out her phone. She's about to do it when she stops. 'Do you think we should call the police?'

This just got real. Maybe we *should* call the police. I am so scared and I need this feeling to go away. I nod at Obi. 'Find a police officer,' I say. There are loads of them around tonight. 'Tell them everything.'

Obi is about to run off when she stops.

'What?'

'Did you hear that?' she asks.

I listen hard. My ears are ringing from the fireworks, but there's something else – screaming.

Tara!

It's coming from the common. We both start sprinting, we round the corner and the common looks so dark. I don't want to go on to it, but there is a shape about twenty metres away. Whoever it is, they're wearing a cloak. I'm so relieved to have found Tara . . . but the way she's dancing around is not good – like she's in pain.

She screams again.

'Tara!' I shout, and somehow I run even faster. 'We're coming.'

I see a shadow racing away from Tara. Gerry. What's she done to her?

Tara's still twirling around, pulling at something on her neck. 'Help me!' she screams.

There is smoke rising from her back. Oh God, Gerry's set her on fire!

I get to Tara and she's freaking out, pulling at the clasp of the cape around her neck.

'Help me, Abby!' she screams. 'Someone put something in my cloak!'

The smoke is coming from her hood.

'It's sizzling,' says Obi, sounding panicked. She looks at me over Tara's shoulder. 'I think she's put a firework in there!'

'Help me!' Tara screams again.

I reach into the hood, but it's too hot. It burns my hands.

I try to undo the chain fastening the cape round Tara's neck. It's got a tricky clasp, and my fingers are clumsy from the cold, and Tara's squirming so much she's making it difficult.

'Stay still,' I whisper. 'I'm going to fix this. But you mustn't move.'

Tara takes a deep breath and goes rigid. I can hear her gulping, the tears streaming down her face as she tries to keep as still as possible. 'Please. Abby, please!'

The clasp on the chain is one where I have to pull back the tiny lever and unhook it so I can slip the chain out. It requires a steady hand, and mine are shaking like mad. But I think to myself, *If Tara can be brave, so can I*. I order my fingers to obey. I unhook the clasp and the cape falls in a heavy smoking heap to the floor.

'Now run!' I grab Tara's hand and sprint. Obi runs the other way. We've only gone about five steps when we hear a series of loud bangs go off – fizzing and shrieking, and movement from the bundle of cape. Tara and I duck behind a bench. Tara's cape is made from such heavy velvet that it weighs the firework down a little. It flies up a few metres and explodes. The sound is deafening and smoke streams from the cloak. It bursts into flames, falls to a heap on the floor, then burns itself out.

I see spots everywhere.

'Tara,' I say, 'are you OK?'

'Yes,' she says, hardly able to speak. 'No. I don't know. I think so.'

I hug her. She's shivering, and I don't think it's because she's cold.

Obi races over to us. 'Are you two all right?'

'Yes!' I call back. 'Are you?'

Obi's nodding as she gets to us. She wraps us in a huge hug.

'What happened?' says Tara. 'I was waiting for you.' She's looking at me. 'Then someone came over wearing an elf mask. I thought it could be you — it wasn't the one you were making before, but I haven't seen you in so long I thought you might have changed it. She didn't say anything. But once she got closer I knew it wasn't you . . . but I didn't know who it was. Then she circled me. I thought she was trying to be funny. But it was really creepy. She just kept walking around me not saying a word even though I asked her who she was. Then she pulled something from her pocket, lit it and shoved it in my hood.'

'It was Gerry,' I say. 'She's insane . . . and not just in a normal way.'

'Abby and I tracked her down last week and it turns out she lied about everything – her name isn't even Gerry!'

'What a freak!' Tara says.

'I'm just glad you're OK,' I say. 'Are you OK?'

Tara nods. Her teeth are chattering.

'We'll find my mum and dad,' I say to Obi. 'Get them to take Tara home and then we'll call the police.'

Obi nods. 'Come on, Tara.'

I take off my coat and give it to Tara. While she's shivering, I can't feel the cold at all. Obi and I go on either side of her and walk her back to the high street. I check my watch. It's been about an hour and my parents will be back where I left them.

'I'll call the others and let them know we've found you,' says Obi.

'Thanks for rescuing me, Abby,' says Tara.

'What are best friends for?' I say. 'If . . . you still want to be my best friend.'

'Forever,' she says, and gives me a hug.

It's possibly the best hug I've ever had. I am so relieved to have Tara back. I don't know what I'd do without her.

We get to the high street and bump into Indiana and Maxie. Tara doesn't even have to say anything to Maxie – Maxie just hugs her tightly. Tara starts sobbing again. She tries to tell her the story through the sobs, and somehow Maxie gets it. They must have a psychic sister thing.

We get to where the fireworks are and it's rammed. I'm just hoping Mum stayed where she said she would. I push past people, they tut at me, but I don't care. I almost cry with relief when I see Dad's back, and Mum smiling up at him.

'Mum! Dad!' I call.

They turn around, beaming from their fun night out. I hate to be the one to ruin it.

As soon as Mum sees my face her smile drops.

'Are you OK?' She catches sight of Maxie with her arm around Tara and Tara looking pale and shivery. 'Tara, sweetheart, what's wrong?'

'Mum, something awful's happened. You need to call the police.'

My dad whips round. 'Is everyone OK?'

'Tara had a lit firework stuck in her hood,' says Obi.

My dad bends so he's eye to eye with Tara. 'Are you hurt?' he asks.

Tara shakes her head.

'Who would do that?' Mum asks.

'It was . . .' I'm about to tell her when I realize that Becky isn't with them. I barely think the question *Where is she?* before I know the answer. 'Who's Becky with?'

Mum brightens a little. 'She's gone off to get a better view of the fireworks. With your lovely friend . . . what's her name?' Mum looks at Dad.

'Gerry,' he says.

And my head spins so fast I almost fall over.
'Then we need to call 999,' Obi says for me.
'What?! Why?' Dad asks.
'Gerry is going to hurt Becky,' I tell him.

Chapter 31

Mum's visibly shaking. Dad can't stop moving his eyes – frantically searching for any sign of his daughter's wheelchair being pushed by a crazy person. He can't spot them. There are too many people.

'Becky needs to take her medication within the next twenty minutes or she could have a seizure,' says Mum. 'I told Gerry that.'

I don't think telling her anything was a good idea. 'What else did you say?'

'That Becky shouldn't eat anything sweet,' she says.

Mum told her exactly how to harm Becky.

'I'm going to look for her,' says Dad, and he's left us before anyone can stop him.

Mum doesn't seem to be able to speak any more – her jaw moves up and down but no sounds come out.

'Obi, you phone the police,' I tell her. 'Mum, you stay here in case – I don't know – in case Becky manages to get away.' Mum nods and starts squeezing her hands together.

'Maxie, call your mum and get her to come and take Tara home – she's in shock.'

Tara sticks her chin in the air. 'I'm fine now. I'm helping.'

'Are you sure?' I ask. 'You don't have to.'

'Are you kidding? I want to get that cow,' she says. 'More than ever.'

'OK,' I say. 'Maxie – call the other girls and tell them we're looking for Gerry and Becky and it's an emergency.'

Maxie nods.

'Tara,' I say. Tara stands beside me. 'Let's go.'

Mum calls after me as we run off down the street again – I think she's telling me to come back, but I'm not listening. It was me that brought Gerry into our lives, it's me who'll get rid of her.

'Where do you think she'd take her?' Tara asks.

'I don't know.' Everything I thought I knew

329

about Gerry was made up. I only know what she wanted me to. 'She'll have gone somewhere away from people,' I say, and that's all I can know for sure.

We race back down the high street, this time calling for Becky. Tara asks the people we pass if they've seen a girl in a wheelchair being pushed by another girl dressed like an elf. They point in the vague direction of the common again. Of course she would take her there – it's quiet. She can do what she likes and there'll be no one around to stop her.

We get back to the common – the scene of the hideous crime Gerry pulled on Tara just minutes ago. She's not around. But it's so dark it's hard to see anything.

I shove down my fear of the dark and stride out on to the common. 'Becky!' I shout.

I think I hear a reply. Just half an 'Ab—' before it gets muffled.

'This way!' I say to Tara.

The noise came from the middle of the common. Where the pond is. The *big* pond. Big enough to drown a girl in a wheelchair.

And as we get closer I see the shadowy forms: Becky in her wheelchair, Gerry behind her. They are way too close to the water's edge.

'Becky!' I yell, hardly able to breathe.

Becky smiles at me. Weirdly, so does Gerry. But her eyes are wide and terrifying.

'Hi, Abby! Hey, Tara,' says Becky. She waves. 'Gerry's here,' she says. 'Isn't that cool? She's brought me some sweets.'

'Don't eat them!' I yell.

'These are Gerry's special sweets,' she says, looking up at her with adoration. 'No sugar. They're fine for me to have.'

I'd bet my life they aren't. I turn to Tara, hand her my phone and whisper, 'Call the police, call an ambulance, call my dad and mum – in that order.'

Gerry is smirking.

Even after everything that's happened, I can't believe she'd actually harm my innocent sick little sister just to get at me. 'Rebecca, do *not* eat those sweets,' I say, sounding as big sisterly as possible.

Gerry whispers something into Becky's ear and makes Becky laugh.

'What did you say?' I ask Gerry.

'I told her not to listen to you. You say stuff . . . but you don't mean it. Stuff about sweets, about your friends, and best friends. It's probably a lie.'

After all the massive lies Gerry's told, and she's still mad at me for my little white one! I walk towards them slowly. One push and Becky could end up in the pond. Behind me, Tara's making the calls but this doesn't seem to phase Gerry.

'I understand, Gerry,' I say, creeping forward. 'I hurt you and I'm sorry for lying. But please don't involve Becky in all this. She's still not very well.'

'Ha, funny. That's what you said before . . . and it turned out she was fine. Another lie.'

'That doesn't mean she's OK. Those sweets are really bad for her. She needs her medication soon or else she could have a fit. I need to take her back to my parents.'

Gerry backs away from me. 'No. You're not going.'

'Why are you doing this?' I say to her. 'You are a really fun girl to be around. You are nice — or . . . you can be. And generous.' I think of the stuff she stole for me — a warped kind of generosity, but she meant it in the right way. 'And really caring. You were so kind when Becky got sick on holiday. I'm grateful.'

'Not grateful enough to be my friend,' she spits out bitterly. Becky looks up at her, suddenly getting that things aren't as fun as she thought they were.

'I definitely wanted you as a friend,' I say. 'I just . . . already had a *best* friend.' I look back at Tara who is making phone calls in the darkness. 'I could never have another one.'

'Then you should have said so!' Gerry says, and her voice catches. I'm almost beside her now. Despite everything, she looks so miserable I'm tempted to give her a hug.

'I tried but—'

'Abby . . .' says Becky, her voice a little slurred. 'I don't feel well.' The moonlight on her face makes her look really pale. She shuts her eyes.

Oh God, she needs her medication. Now.

'Becky!' I shout, and crouch by her side. 'Oh my God! Tara, where's that ambulance?'

She doesn't have to answer as the sound of sirens comes blaring up the roads surrounding the common.

I jump up and I'm about to grab the wheelchair to race her towards the ambulance when it's snatched away from me.

'No!' Gerry shouts.

Becky starts groaning. 'Abby,' she says. 'It's really bad.'

'Give her to me!' I say to Gerry.

'No,' she says, 'she's mine.'

I lunge forward but Gerry's too quick. She pulls Becky away and then grabs me by my ponytail. It hurts, but I'm only thinking about Becky – she could have a seizure any moment. Gerry has one hand on my ponytail, holding me back, and the other on Becky's wheelchair, keeping it away from me.

'Let me go!' I say. 'This is not how you make friends. You have to let me go.'

Gerry doesn't say anything. Instead she lets

go of Becky's wheelchair, which starts rolling slowly towards the edge of the pond.

'Tara!' I shout. Tara drops the phone from her ear and runs, but she's too far away to stop it from happening. Becky's rolling forward. Gerry is reaching into her pocket for something while pulling my hair so hard I can't move. It's something shiny. A blade! Oh God, she's going to kill me! If I die, how will I save my sister?

Then I see that Gerry's holding a pair of scissors. She brings them up to my face. I close my eyes and wait for the cut.

But suddenly I feel a tearing sensation and a release. I'm free to lurch forward, and I'm lying full stretch across the muddy ground. The front wheels of Becky's wheelchair are over the side of the pond but I manage to grab a metal bar at the back.

I've saved my sister.

I look back at Gerry. She has something in her hand. At first I think it's something to hit me with, but then I realize it's my ponytail.

She's cut my hair off.

Behind Gerry I see adults running towards us.

The flashing lights behind them let me know it's the police and the ambulance. Tara is beside me now. She pulls Becky safely away from the edge of the pond so I can move. I scramble to my feet.

'Help her!' I shout. 'My sister needs her medication!'

The police slow down as they get to us, but the paramedics don't. They rush straight to Becky.

'She's got a kidney condition. She—'

'We know,' the lady says as she checks Becky's pulse. 'Your friend told us on the phone.'

Tara holds my hand. We don't take our eyes off Becky. I'm so glad Tara's with me now. We watch as the paramedics check Becky over. With them here, I know she's going to be OK.

The police approach Gerry. 'Are you Gerry Barnes?'

'Her real name is Sophie Ross,' I tell them. 'She . . .' I'm not sure where to start. I touch the back of my head where my long hair used to be.

'Did you take this young girl away from her parents?'

Gerry clenches her teeth. The darkness she's shown so many times is there for everyone to see. I saw it in that very first week. Why didn't I take it as a warning?

'She put a firework in the hood of my cloak,' says Tara. 'It's over there somewhere.' She points over towards the edge of the common where we left the burnt remains of Tara's costume.

'I . . .' says Gerry. She looks at me and Tara and Becky, still looking sick and in need of her meds. 'She stole too,' Gerry points at me. 'She's as big a thief as I am.'

I don't care who knows now. I don't care what happens to me. 'I did. I shoplifted a chocolate bar.' I look at the police. 'Arrest me if you like, but just get this girl away. She's dangerous.'

All eyes turn to Gerry.

Her dark look is finally gone. She knows it's all over. 'I want to go home,' she says, and she sounds like a child.

The policemen steer her towards the police van. 'You're coming to the police station,' I hear him say as they go.

I wonder what will happen to her. Gerry clearly has a lot of problems. I hope the police and her social worker find a way to make her feel better so she doesn't feel the need to possess people like she tried to possess me.

I see two more people racing over.

They rush to Becky's side, Mum frantically getting her medication out from her bag.

Tara puts her arm around me. 'Are *you* OK?' she whispers. She strokes my uneven hair.

I don't know *what* I am.

I brought a psychopath into our lives. I liked the way she made me feel different to who I was. But that was the problem – I wasn't being myself. I'm not flabby or boring, I'm me. And I can be fun with or without Gerry. But what I do know is that I'm not myself without Tara. She's too much a part of my life.

My guess is, Sophie saw herself losing her friend Ellie Poole when Ellie got a boyfriend, and she felt desperate. And I can relate – I drew that picture of Tara when she started dating Reece, something I hate myself for now . . . I regret it even more than the shoplifting. Sophie needs help to get herself whatever she feels is missing in her life. I really hope the social worker can do that for her. If Sophie copied the woman's name – Gerry Barnes – I'm guessing she's all right.

Sophie needs some love and support. If only she had a group of friends like the Boys' School Girls. If only she had a best friend like Tara.

'If only she had a best friend,' Tara says.

And at that moment I realize that there was always someone who thought I was cool – even before Gerry came along. She says it to me so often that I stopped hearing it. Tara never thought of me as Boring Flabby Abby. I took it for granted that Tara loved me. And I took Tara for granted too. I'm never going to let that happen again.

'Just wait till I tell Joel about this,' she adds.

But right now, I don't care about Joel. I need to feel secure and safe, and the person who's always made me feel that way is Tara. No matter how long it takes for Becky to get better, or how long we have to wait before a suitable kidney donor comes up, Tara will be there for me. I'm forgetting about boys and everything else except our friendship for a while.

As my parents concentrate on Becky, who's

getting her medication and being put into the ambulance, I realize that Tara has *always* been the one there holding my hand whenever there's a crisis. She's the one I can always count on.

My best friend.

I'm never going to forget it again.

THE END

Look out for Lil Chase's other brilliant books!

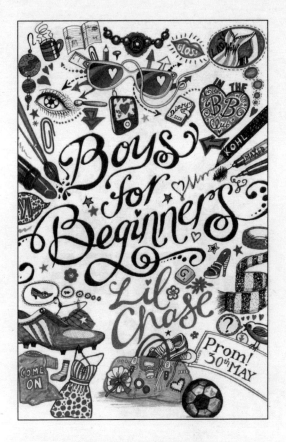

Gwynnie thought all boys were a
waste of time – until Charlie
started at her school . . .

Quercus
www.lilchase.com

Look out for Lil Chase's other brilliant books!

What would you do if you knew
the deepest, darkest secrets
of everyone in school?

Quercus
www.lilchase.com